CONVICTION

NYC Doms

JANE HENRY

FREE READ!

Sign up for Jane's newsletter and get a free read! Sign up *HERE*.

CONVICTION (NYC Doms)
By: Jane Henry

Copyright 2018 by Jane Henry

Please do not share or distribute in any way.

Chapter 1

Braxton

I'M PRETTY sure it's a total dickhead move to mentally undress the woman on the dance floor in front of me, but, you know, love is in the air and all that shit, so I don't much care. I came here to toast the happy couple who, like *smart people,* went and eloped months ago. Their friends were a little miffed they didn't get a chance to celebrate, so once spring came Zack and Bea announced they were having a reception. I'm always game for something that involves free food and liberal amounts of beer, so here I am, even dressed in a fucking suit which hasn't happened since… ok, ever.

But Jesus, this woman's gorgeous, and likely young enough to make even looking at her illegal, but who's gonna stop me? She's got a dancer's blood in her veins or something, because this girl has *moves*. As the music pumps through speakers so loudly I feel it in my bones, her hips grind in time to the beat, and it's fucking beautiful. I'm half in awe of her energy, unable to take my eyes off her. Though she's all round curves—petite but voluptuous, her creamy shoulders bare, the sleeveless short dress she's wearing clearly being held up my magic—she's got edges, too. I can tell just looking at her there's a ferocity that fuels her. On her right shoulder she's got a tattoo of a bird in flight. While I watch her dance, I fantasize about sinking my teeth into that tattoo, then smacking my hand against her curvy, gorgeous ass. She shakes her head, the thick locks of chestnut-colored hair loosening, little tendrils clinging to her damp forehead as she gets down to the music. The beat gyrates around me as she wiggles her hips, her feet moving in time to the crazy-ass beat.

"Hey, Brax, have you seen Diana?" My friend Tobias comes up to me and taps my beer bottle with his. Diana, his wife and Beatrice's best friend, toasted the happy couple, but I haven't seen her since.

"No, man," I say, shaking my head. I take another swig of my beer, then watch the girl in front of me as she snags one of her friends around the waist and they dance together. Christ. One was bad enough. Two of them dancing together? I'll leave this place with fucking blue balls.

"Get it out of your head, man," Tobias says. "Can't get your eyes off Zoe? That won't end well for you. Don't even entertain the thought." Tobias is technically my boss, but also my friend, and though I trust his judgment, I don't hear warning in his tone but a dare.

"Yeah?" I ask, watching her even more intently now.

"Braxton," he says warningly.

"What? Dude, you can't just say 'stop looking at the most gorgeous woman in this room and forget about her' and expect me be all, 'yeah, sounds right, whatever you say.' Did you forget who I am?"

Tobias sobers then. He leans against the bar, crossing his arms on his chest, and fixes me with a serious look. His dark brown eyes, shadowed by a shock of dark brown hair that falls on his forehead, darken. "That's one of Zack's best friends, and she's an officer with the NYPD. She's easily ten years younger than you, and I don't know much, but I know that girl has got a *shit ton* of baggage."

Who doesn't? The idea of that woman kicking the crap out of someone makes her that much more attractive to me. And Jesus. Baggage? That doesn't dissuade me. I live in fucking New York City. There's no such thing as a New Yorker without baggage. Hell, I'm a classic example. I sold my auto body shop this past winter when a friend offered me a job that paid a hell of a lot more than I was currently earning. I'm a full time Dungeon Monitor at Tobias's club, Verge, and I make good money there. Picking up some private work on the side has supplemented my income, and hell I need it, because Devin does, and child support doesn't go on sale. The thought of my six-year-old daughter almost sobers me, then the music shifts and Zoe's back at it again.

"Everyone's got baggage, man," I say to Tobias. "You know I'm no exception."

He shakes his head. "Brax, there's baggage and then there's *baggage*. She's beautiful, but she doesn't know shit about the lifestyle, and if you touch a hair on her head, Beatrice or Zack, or possibly even both of them, will kick your ass. They've gotten tight."

Beatrice is like five foot nothing and now married to the sternest Dom in all of Verge. That's supposed to scare me? I know Zack won't care.

"Fuck," Tobias says, watching me with narrowed eyes as I finish my beer and plunk the empty on the counter. "Don't say I didn't warn you."

I grin at him. "Challenge accepted."

Chapter 2

oe

I throw back another shot of Fireball, the sweet, fiery liquid coursing down my throat and into my gut, my head deliciously light and my body practically floating. I'm starting to feel a little woozy, but it's a feeling I've gotten comfortable with. I've somehow managed to obliterate the memories that plague me and after a while, all that shit blends together into one big mess of pain that I seek to blur with alcohol. I'm responsible enough to never drink on the job, of course, and I'm a normal, law-abiding citizen. But on a night of celebration like this? I let things go because I'll grab a cab home.

I'm happy as I can be for Beatrice and Zack but seeing how he is with her leaves me a little wistful. He looks at her as if she's the most precious thing he's ever laid eyes on, his treasure.

I'm not into Zack. Not that way. We're nothing but buddies, and I trust the man with my life. Even though he's moved up on the force and become a detective, we're still tight. So it isn't him that I want, or even Beatrice that I'm jealous of. I want what they have, and it stings being alone. So tonight? I drink. I'll blur the memories of the past that keep me up at night and numb the pain with shot after shot.

I'm off duty, so tonight, I answer to no one. Tomorrow, my head might ache, but tonight I'll rule the world.

And then I see him. He towers over me, all brawn and muscle, dressed in a light blue shirt that matches his eyes, his head is shaved, giving him an edge that makes my pulse race. His gaze meets mine across the room, and he grins at me, a dimple forming in his cheek.

God, I want to lick that dimple.

Without conscious thought, I shift my body so as I dance to the music, I dance for *him*, my hips swaying, chest heaving. I love dancing and always have, but it takes a few drinks to get me into it. I watch as he uncrosses his arms. Excitement curls in my belly as he prowls toward me. I quickly glance over my shoulder. Is he looking at someone else? He has to be. Someone who's… pretty.

But there's just a couple dancing with their backs to me, and when I turn back to him, I can tell he's laughing by the way his shoulders quake. He shakes his head from side to side and points an index finger directly at me. By now he's close enough I can hear what he says.

"No, baby. *You.*"

Baby? A shiver of excitement courses through me. No one ever calls me baby. Jesus, I need another shot. He's so close now I can see his eyes are a sapphire blue, he has not one but *two* dimples, and he's way, way bigger than I thought at first. I have to crane my neck to look up at him, which is kinda hard to do since I'm still dancing. He steps closer to me, slings his huge hand to the small of my back, and without a word, pulls me to him. When his hand touches me, a vibration of lust thrums through my body, his touch firm and possessive. We dance as if this song had been written for us, choreographed with precision, my steps in time with his, our bodies a crush of heat and tension that thrills me.

He grabs my hand and spins me out, and I twirl, feeling like a princess for the three seconds it takes him to spin me back into him, the beat of the music *booming* through my body like thunder. With a sharp tug, my body brushes his from torso to hips. His touch is possessive, his heat magnetic, and I suddenly need to kiss him before the music stops.

I meet his eyes boldly, get up on my tiptoes, and wrap my hands around his massive shoulders. He doesn't need any more of a hint. Our movements slow and the music seems to slow with them, the crowd fading as he wraps his hand around the back of my neck and pulls my hair back, a sharp tug I feel all the way between my thighs, my panties already damp.

What the hell is he doing? No man has ever touched me like this. My mouth falls open with a gasp, and he makes his move, claiming my mouth with his. My heart hammers so loudly I swear it rivals the music. Lights flash behind my eyes. I blame the whiskey, but this moment is like it was lifted straight out of a movie, and I don't want it to end.

His tongue, hot and insistent, traces the edge of my lower lip. I have no power over myself, and yield without conscious thought, melting into him, my body sliding easily against his. I realize with a shock, I don't even know his name. Who am I? Where are we?

I'm on a rollercoaster and I can't get off, too caught up in the speed and force of my heart. The heat of his body turns my insides to liquid as he draws a moan from somewhere deep inside me. When he pulls away I whimper at the loss, grasping his shoulders as I stand on tiptoe, my eyes meeting his blue ones in shock, arousal, and wonder.

"Who are you?" I whisper through swollen lips, my voice strangely slurred and husky. He only grins, those two adorable dimples making my heart flutter in my chest.

"You first," he says. "Your name?"

"Zoe," I breathe.

He bends his head down so he can hear me. "Zoe?" He chuckles. "Of course it is. A name as cute as the woman owning it. I'm Brax."

"Thanks," I say with a smile, then a flash of white over his shoulder catches my attention. It's Beatrice, wearing a fitted white dress and waving her hand at me, her eyes as wide as saucers. The room spins a little, and I'm vaguely aware of alarm in her eyes. She mouths something, but we're so far apart I couldn't catch it even if I was sober. She throws back her head back in exasperation and whips out a cell phone, pointing her finger at it. A second later, my phone buzzes in my pocket. I blow her a kiss and turn my back to her.

"Getting kinda hot in here," he says, and even though it's such a classic pick-up line, I fall like an anchor thrown overboard. I'm sunk, and I'm not resurfacing now. "You wanna go someplace quiet where we can talk?"

"Can we still dance?" I ask coyly.

"Yeah, baby. I'll take you to where we can dance." He reaches for my hand, warm and strong and secure. I can't help it. A little part of me yearns for that, and I pull a little closer to him without meaning to. "But Zoe, one thing you need to know."

"Yeah?"

He pulls me away from the crowd, toward a deserted hallway. My phone buzzing like crazy but I silence it.

Leaning in, his deep voice tickles my ear. "If you're

with me, the only one you dance like that for is *me*. You get me?"

I laugh like a woman possessed and trot to keep up with his long strides. "Oh yeah," I agree, realizing that I'm leaving the party with a stranger.

When we got out of the crush of people and into the hallway, I shiver a little. I'd gotten used to the warmth, being surrounded by others, and the vacant hall holds a chill.

"You got a coat or something?"

"Oh, somewhere, I think," I say, waving a vague hand in the general direction of the coat closet. My mind is a weird haze of confusion, and I can't for the life of me remember what I brought with me or where I put it. I have my wristlet and my phone, so I'm not really forgetting anything terribly important.

"You think?" he asks, eyeing me curiously.

"I've, um, had a few shots."

He chuckles. "I can see that."

"And my memory's a little... shall we say... *hazy.*"

"Uh huh. So do you mean to tell me that tomorrow you'll forget we even met?"

No. No, Mister Mystery Man, no one would ever forget those blue eyes or dimples or the way your voice slides over me like silk.

"I don't know," I say, an uncharacteristic note of flirtation in my voice. "Depends on how memorable you make this night."

He laughs out loud, a deep, booming laugh that startles me a bit, but at the same time he draws me close. I hardly have time to feel cold before I relax into his warmth. *Be careful*, a little voice in my head says. Then I remember Beatrice.

"Before we go, I need to hit the ladies' room, okay?"

He nods. "Sure." Leading me to the hallway where the doors to the restrooms are, he releases my hand and leans up against the wall. "I'll wait."

I practically skip into the bathroom, slide into a stall, and quickly latch it. I can't make yet another stupid, brash decision when under the influence. God, I can't. Not again. I glance quickly at the phone.

ZOE. YOU DO NOT LEAVE THIS PARTY WITH HIM. THAT'S BRAX.

Wait. What?

Frowning, I text back. *Seriously? Why not? He seems really nice.*

He is nice! Came the immediate reply. *He's just into stuff you are not into!*

What the fuck is that supposed to mean? We aren't buying a house together. I have honestly no idea *what* we we're doing together, but it's nothing serious.

Don't worry about it. Is he Zack's friend?

Beatrice's husband is, hands down, the most responsible guy ever. He's my friend, and as straight-laced as humanly possible. If Brax is Zack's friend, I trust him.

Well yes, but…

I sigh impatiently. *But what?*

But I'm not sure he's your type.

And that right there angers me. I am so sick of people telling me what to do. Beatrice just stood in front of a roomful of people with the man of her dreams on her arm, the real deal, the kinda guy that puts you on a pedestal and treats you like a princess. I don't begrudge her in the least, but where does she get off trying to dissuade me from doing… whatever it is I'm doing. Sudden tears blur my vision.

I'm not sure you know my type.

Do I?

And with that, I shut my phone off, shove it in my bag, and stalk over to the sink, wobbling a little. I wash my hands and tidy my hair, which looks oddly askew. The whole outfit does, weirdly. The mirror seems a little lopsided, the light at an odd angle, and I wonder what the hell they did to it, or if something is wrong with me.

I'm on my way out to do… things I shouldn't do… with a man I not only don't know, but who Beatrice has just told me to run away from.

Fuck that. I run a lip gloss brush over my lips, and a brush through my dark brown hair. My eyes are bright and excited, and there's a pink flush to my cheeks that I rarely see.

So Brax is into *things I'm not into*.

I can deal.

As I leave the bathroom, a weirdly irrational thought comes to mind: What if he left? What if he found another girl, a prettier girl?

Why do I care?

But when I push open the door to the restroom, he's leaning up against the wall, one foot propped up, his hands in his pockets. He's sexy as sin and my heart goes thumping like mad. He's there. He waited for me. And the night is young.

He tosses me a lopsided grin, one corner of his lips quirking up. "Ready, babe?"

I grin back in return.

"I'm so ready."

I ignore the small buzz of foreboding in my stomach. Beatrice my instant-conscience chides me from my shoulder, but I tell her to shut up. Just for tonight. I love her but her voice in my head's being a pain in the ass.

"Want to get a drink somewhere?" I ask him.

He pushes open the door and gestures for me to go

through. Jesus, that's nice. No one does that anymore. Maybe in some small town in the south or something but here, in NYC? No way.

"Why thank you," I say, walking through the door. He follows behind me, the brisk spring wind blowing my hair askew. I giggle as it sticks in my lip gloss and I whip my head around so my hair flows behind me.

"Drink?" he says. "Yeah, maybe some coffee. Not sure you need any more alcohol."

God. Did I just end up with a prude or something? But no. Prudes don't dance like he danced with me on that floor. Still, it sorta pisses me off that he thinks it's cool to tell me I've had enough to drink.

"You my keeper tonight?" I ask, an edge in my voice. I wrap my arms around myself, and it surprises me when he comes up next to me, tugs one arm free, and nabs my hand. As we walk, he pulls me close to him so that he's between me and the street and I'm nearest the buildings.

"Did you just walk out of a club with a guy you don't know?" he asks.

Well, yeah, I did.

"Beatrice says you're friends with Zack," I say, feeling defensive. "Any friend of Zack's is a friend of mine."

He snickers. "Weird logic, babe. Answer the question." Now *his* voice holds an edge, and I wonder where he's going with this.

"Well, yeah."

"Then yes. You walked out of that party with me, therefore that makes me your keeper. For now. And I saw you tossing back those shots like they were water. So let's do something else instead of destroying our livers."

I snort. Jesus. "Are you for real?"

And before I know what's happening, he tugs my wrist

and pulls me close, with one fluid motion pinning me up against the brick wall of the building behind us. My instincts war with my desire to be dominated. I'm a fighter. I could have this man sprawling on the ground in front of me and begging for mercy if I wanted to, but I love the way my heart races. I love the way I feel small and subdued like this. He doesn't know who I am. I eye his large form. A quick duck and knee to the groin area would have him groaning and incapacitated in seconds, but I have to remind myself that he's not my aggressor. This is something way different, and hell… better.

I blink up at him. His arms are on either side of me, caging me in, and his blue eyes are locked with mine. He's huge and he smells so fucking good my mouth practically waters. I'm not used to men like this. I'm the one in charge, calling the shots, and making sure that men fucking respect me. I swear to God I can't even remember the last time I was with a guy. There's a teasing glint in his look, but a hint of steel I can't deny. My head spins like I just stepped off a merry-go-round.

He leans in and whispers in my ear. "Yeah, babe. Question is, are you gonna do what you're told or not?"

My heart flutters even as my mind reels with how wrong this is. "And if I don't?" I whisper. There's something about him that says *danger* and I fucking love it, like toeing the edge of a cliff, or standing by train tracks with the approaching screech of metal on metal rumbling in the distance warning me. Danger's so close I can taste it, but I love the way it makes my heart race. How I feel so damn *alive*.

He shakes his head with a hint of regret that makes my panties dampen. God, I need this. "If you don't? Then I might have to *make* you."

I feel my insides clench in warning.

Beatrice warned me. Was this what she was warning me about?

I lick my lips, my mouth suddenly dry. "Oh yeah?" I whisper.

And then I know: I want him to make me.

A siren sounds in the distance, a crowd of people walk past us laughing and jostling each other, and far away a dog barks, but all I can focus on is the sound of his breathing and mine. I swallow hard and blink, but then decide I'm gonna make this happen. I've never once had a one-night stand but hell, something tells me this guy will make it worth it.

I slide under his arms pressed on either side of me, gently nudge him back, grab his shirt and tug him down to me. He looks at me in surprise, but I don't wait, I fling my hands around the back of his head and tug his beautiful, gorgeous mouth down to mine and kiss him hard. He moans, pushing his body closer to mine, but within seconds I realize it's because he's taking back control, backpedaling me, and my wrists are pinned to my sides. My heart races, and I don't know if it's the alcohol, the excitement, or fear —maybe all of the above—but I lose my mind a little. Wriggling my wrists free, I pretend to reach out to hug him, then reach around slap his beautiful, perfect ass. The sound reverberates around us like the clanging of a gong, and his whole body tightens. His blue eyes darken and he seems… dangerously amused.

"You just slapped the ass of a dominant, sweetheart."

A… what?

A nervous giggle bubbles up without my consent, but the giggle is soon swallowed in the wind as he dips down, tucks his shoulder into my belly, and lifts me straight up in the air and *over his shoulder* like a caveman. I half expect him to roar and pound his chest or drag me by the hair and call me *woman* in grunts.

Holy shit! What the hell is he doing?

"Ahhhhhh!" I scream, but he silences me with a firm but teasing swat on the rear, and I swear the smack goes straight to my sex. I halfheartedly whack his back, but I don't really try to stop him because I don't really want to.

"You like ass smacking, Zoe?" he asks. "Lucky for you, I know of a place where you'll fit right in. We're close to my stomping grounds."

What? What's he talking about?

"I was teasing you!" I protest, wiggling like puppy, but his huge arm traps my legs, his voice rumbling over my protests.

"Stop that." He's more serious than I've heard him yet, and now I begin to wonder what's going on here, but my mind is still hazy.

"Where are we going?" I ask, but he doesn't say anything, just takes these huge, massive strides that bring us to a shiny black door. With his free hand, he turns the knob and pushes it open, then lowers his shoulder and slides me down his chest to the floor. With my body pressed up against his, I can feel his latent power, and my core contracts with heat and arousal. Some big, muscled guy is standing in the doorway, and his brows shoot up in surprise.

"Master Braxton," the guy says.

Um. *Master*?

"Evenin'," Brax says, taking me by the hand and tugging me into some sorta community room with loveseats and padded chairs.

"Where the hell are we? And why did he just call you *master?*"

Brax sits heavily on a chair, nabs my wrist, and in a

matter of seconds has me belly down over his knee. He slides one hand through my hair and tugs my head back.

"Club Verge is a BDSM Club. I'm a member."

I can't think much beyond a startled *Jesus* as he continues.

"You like smacking my ass?" he says in my ear, his voice deep, his breath warm against my sensitized skin. A delicious shiver runs through me, and I swear I can hardly think, then *his* hand smacks my ass, a good sharp crack that takes my breath away and *holy hell that's hot*.

"Umm," I mumble, closing my eyes against the heat that washes over me. I have no idea where I am, and I feel strangely like I should. This isn't my jurisdiction and NYC's friggin' huge, so I don't know where I am, and I have no idea where this night's gonna lead. I only have the vaguest idea what a BDSM Club even is. But, for some reason, I trust this guy that I hardly know, and Beatrice's warning only makes this hotter.

"I asked you a question," he corrects, his voice tightening and somehow more serious than before, a note of authority that makes my spine prickle.

"Apparently not," I whisper.

"We do not go through that door unless you're with me. You're my guest here. I'm dungeon monitor, and this is one of the most renowned kink clubs in NYC which means there are rules."

A nervous giggle bubbles up. "No shit?"

He chuckles and pulls my hair a little harder. "No shit." A beat passes. "We go past these doors, you need to trust me. When you wake up tomorrow and your head's clear, I don't want you to regret this. So think before you answer. You with me, Zoe?"

Am I with him? This is the most exciting thing I've done in months and now this hot guy who makes fire pulse through my veins wants to bring me to his club where he's like all powerful? Even the tone of his voice now is doing crazy sexy things to my body. Ha. I don't need to think twice. I'm not reasoning with my head now anyway.

"Yeah," I say, my words are in some kinda tunnel. "I'm with you." I figure it's because I haven't been laid in *a year* and my body is primed like embers in a glowing fire, ready to ignite. He grins, gets to his feet, and leads me toward the door that looks like an entryway, and just as we go to enter, a couple clad in all leather wearing so many piercings I can hardly see skin, comes out the door.

"Master Brax," the girl says, and the guy nods his greeting with a polite, "Sir."

That sobers me up a little, when I'm reminded that the people here call him things like *master* and *sir*, but it's also hot as hell in a weird, sorta scary way. We enter through the door, and I'm skipping to keep up with his long strides. People recognize him as we walk, nodding and saying hello, but he just grunts and nods, clearly on a mission to get out of the crush of people. This place looks fun, though.

"Hey! Hey, there's a bar. Buy me a drink, master?" I snicker at my own joke, but he only purses his lips and walks faster.

Walking me through a hallway, the noise dims and now my heartbeat really does kick up. Where are we going? What exactly have I agreed to? There's a vibrant green door all the way down at the end of the hall. Still holding my hand, with his free hand he takes a set of keys out of his pocket and slides it through the keyhole. He pushes the door open.

"This is my room here," he says. Without another word, he shuts and locks the door behind us and pockets the key. I look around curiously. There's an enormous bed in the center of the room piled high with pillows, a wardrobe, a little refrigerator, and to the side, a doorway to what looks like a bathroom. There are throw rugs on the floor, a little loveseat in one corner of the room and lots of space. But there are other things I've never seen before, some leather-looking things hanging from the wall and little contraptions made of metal. But I don't have time to look at much, as he's already sitting on the edge of the bed and pulling me between his knees.

He tugs my hair back and kisses me, slow and sweet at first, as if asking permission. God, I want to forget everything tonight. I want to feel and live this in the moment, get totally swept away in the spontaneity of it all.

He pulls his mouth off mine long enough to grunt, "Christ, you're gorgeous."

"Uh huh, sure," I say, without even thinking of what I'm saying. "You must be drunker than I am."

With a low growl, his knees part and he tugs me straight over one of them so that my body is on the bed and my pussy is pressed up against his knee. Before I know what he's doing, his hand cracks down on my ass with a wicked *slap!* First one, then two hard smacks land.

It hurts but feels so damn good that I give myself over to whatever the hell he's doing. A dim part of my brain says, *Hey, wait a minute, he's spanking you,* but I don't really care because all I wanna do right now is feel, and *hell* do I ever.

"Say you're beautiful," he orders. The hazy fog in my mind clears and I wonder where he's going with this.

"What?"

His response is another good ass smack that zings right to my core, which pulses as if his hand is magically connected to my pussy.

"You heard me."

Another spank has me gasping for air. "Okay. I'm beautiful!" I say, following his instruction before shit gets real. I may be totally plastered and riding the waves of excitement here, but I'm no fool. I'm over the knee of a man twice my size with a palm of steel, and he's telling me what to do, so like a smart girl, I do what he says.

He tosses me up onto the bed. "Confidence is sexy, sweetheart," he says, kneeling over me and taking both my wrists in hand, placing them above my head, then his mouth comes down to my neck and he suckles the skin there like he's starving, and I'll stave his hunger. I moan and wiggle, but he's got me trapped. "Say it again."

"I'm beautiful," I breathe, and I know it's a lie. I'm fat and my boobs are weird and my belly's flabby, but somehow, saying the words, hearing him draw them out from me, for one brief minute I believe them. "I'm beautiful," I breathe again, hoping that I'll earn another luscious swipe of his tongue on my sensitized skin.

"Good girl," he says. "You're gorgeous, and I want to kiss my way down those lush curves of yours until you melt like ice cream on a summer day."

I giggle at the analogy. "I could deal with that."

He releases my wrists and his mouth comes to my shoulder, his teeth grazing the tat there. "I've wanted to bite that tattoo ever since I saw you on that dance floor."

"You're crazy," I say with a giggle, but Jesus he's my kinda crazy. He lowers himself to me, his mouth at my ear.

"Am I?"

"I'm on birth control," I choke stupidly, needing him to know this has to go further. That I need to be fucked tonight, not wooed or charmed or any other fucking respectful thing.

"Excellent," he breathes, reaching for his wallet. "Still, we don't take risks." He slips a condom out of his wallet, places it next to him, then strips down to his boxers.

"Dress off, Zoe." His voice is husky and deep, and I realize then that this man wants me. *He wants me.* And hell, if that isn't sexy as fuck. "Now, babe."

I do what he says like a trained puppy, my body having a mind of its own.

Tonight, I'm going to forget everything.

Just for tonight.

Chapter 3

Braxton

The light shines through the bottom of the window where the shade doesn't quite meet the windowsill, reminding me it's morning. Zoe's tucked up against me, her voluptuous, full ass pressed against my cock, and damn if she doesn't give me morning wood. She's lightly snoring, totally dead to the world.

I glance at the time on my phone. Verge should be empty now as only long-term members have access to the private rooms, and everything else has been locked up tight until later today. I've got shit to do, though, an appointment in a few hours and since it's my first time on the job with my Myers, I need to get there on time.

"Morning, sunshine," I say, giving Zoe's bare ass a playful smack.

She grunts, rolls over onto her tummy, and groans. "Noooo. God, that was the best night's sleep I've had in *months*. No fair. I'm not getting up."

God, she's adorable. Her hair is adorably mussed up, pointing in every direction before she pulls a pillow over her head and blocks my view. The sheet's all tangled up in her legs, barely covering her. She's got a swirly heart tat just above her ass, and her full thighs and curvy hips make me even harder.

God, what I wouldn't do to scene with this woman.

I gave her a few smacks to the ass last night, and she responded well. How would she respond to more?

"Zoe. C'mon, babe. You're not in my place or I'd let you sleep in. We're still at the club, and even though we're likely the only ones here, I've got to get you home. Where do you live?"

She mumbles something completely incoherent.

I fist the pillowcase and yank the pillow away. She grasps for it, and turns, her face darkening with anger. "Hey. Give me that!"

"Enough," I say, using the deep, dominant tone submissives usually respond to well. She blinks up at me, and her mouth parts open a little, then she winces at the light streaming in the window.

"Oh God, my head hurts."

"You hungover?"

She closes her eyes and whimpers.

"Babe, how much did you drink?" I start to question the decision I made last night. Was she so shit-faced she couldn't really agree to what we did? *Fuck.*

She shakes her head. "I have no idea."

"More than three shots?" I ask.

She snorts, pulling the sheet up over her head. "Fuck yeah. I had three shots before Bea and Zack even got there." Suddenly, the sheets fly away, and she sits straight up in bed, all wide-eyed. "Oh my God. Zack. *Zack.* I told him I'd go!"

Zack? What the fuck?

"Oh God," she says. She's out of the bed now, scrambling for her clothes, with one hand pushed up against her forehead as if to hold her head in place.

"Hey, wait a minute. Just chill, babe."

"I can't chill! I just remembered I told Zack I'd be there. I've waited four months to make this appointment and I can't miss it. You have no idea. I'm sorry but I can't tell you anything else."

What is she talking about?

"You're hungover and don't even know where you are," I say. "At least let me get you something for your headache?" I feel responsible, since I was the douchebag who fucked a drunk girl.

She pauses and when her eyes meet mine, though the look is brief, I see something I hadn't seen before, something that breaks my heart a little. "You're a good guy, you know that? Please, yes, I would love some pain relievers."

"Can I take you somewhere? Hail a cab?"

She pulls on her panties, bra, and dress, her fingers clumsy. I reach for the top of her dress and help her shimmy it up over her breasts. She's hot as hell and I'm hard again just looking at her, but I've gotta help her out.

"Yes, please," she says. "I have to get back to my place and figure things out."

"Sounds good," I say. I pull on my own clothes, then grab my phone and dial a cab. Ten minutes later, we're standing outside Verge and the cab pulls up. She's taken the meds I gave her and has two bottles of water in hand.

"Drink those up, Zoe," I tell her. "And when you get home, call me." I take her phone, program my number in, then hand it back to her.

"I will, promise," she says, but her eyes don't meet mine. "Thank you, Brax." Her voice shakes a little, and I wonder why.

I open the door to the cab, and watch as she slides in.

"Bye, Zoe," I say, a sense of finality hitting me in the gut when the door shuts. She isn't gonna call me. I know she isn't. My phone rings as the cab pulls away, and I have a weird sense of loss. She's waving at me but not looking in my direction, like a celebrity followed by Paparazzi.

I've had many one-night stands, and I can't afford to have anything serious right now. So why does what I just did feel so wrong? With a sigh I answer my phone. "Yeah, Braxton here."

"Brax." It's Stefan Myers, the guy I'm meeting with late this morning to pursue my next job. After I sold the body shop when the hours there and at Verge started to pile on this past winter, Myers was recruiting. He's a high school friend of mine and a private investigator. When he found out I was a bouncer and dungeon master at Verge, he suggested a proposition. What I later found out was they needed more brawn than brains for their operation, and Zack, who's an NYPD detective, gave me a strong recommendation.

Today's my first day on the job.

"What's up, Myers," I say, hailing a cab myself to get to my place so I can get myself together before I meet up with Myers.

"Can you come in earlier?"

"How earlier?"

"Like now."

I blink. I'm still in the rumpled clothing from last night, since I'm not one of those guys who keeps my belongings at Verge. I mentally kick myself for being a dumbass.

"Now?"

"Yeah. Blythe got called in to get his kid at school, and I need someone to handle a client that's on her way in. Can't do it, I'm already off site and won't be back in the office until later."

We haven't talked about much of anything yet, not salary or hours or responsibilities.

"Dude, I'm not sure I'm ready."

"This is just the intake. You meet with the client coming in, you get her information, and you feed that intel to us." He goes on to make me a salary proposition so generous my mouth drops. I'm paid well at Verge but even that pales in comparison.

"No shit?" I ask him, still incredulous.

He chuckles. "No shit."

"Well, yeah, alright. I'm on my way."

"Call me when you get there."

Instead of my home address, I give the taxi driver the address of Myers' private office building, but the whole time I'm wondering if I'll get a text from Zoe. I stare at my phone. Zoe was supposed to call when she arrived safe and sound at home, but the only notification I get is a text from Devin's mom, Nichole. I respond to her as we head to Myers' office. It takes a while to get there as we're now in rush hour NYC traffic.

Zoe doesn't text.

Finally, we get to the office and I'm starting to feel irritated. I'm pissed she didn't even call me, starving since I didn't have breakfast, and really in need of a shower and change of clothes.

We pull up to the massive building, a huge skyscraper with mirrored windows and a doorman. Shit, I don't look like I belong here. I pay the driver, get out of the car, and when my phone buzzes, I look like a kid at the screen, hoping it's Zoe.

Dammit. Nichole again.

I really need the child support early.

Frowning, I reply. *Why? You get it the first of the month and that's in two weeks.*

No response at first. God, I hate this. Nichole and I hooked up when I was still practically a kid myself, and the only good that came out of the whole shit-storm was my beautiful blonde-haired, blue-eyed spitfire of a daughter. Nichole holds the power in this, knows she's got me by the balls because I'll do fucking anything for my kid.

Expenses came up. You have no idea how expensive it is raising a kid in NYC.

I have no idea? I'm the one who buys her clothes and shoes and pays for her dance classes, not to mention the child support. Since Nichole lives with her mom, I know she pays hardly anything for rent.

This isn't about expenses for Devin, but likely something else Nichole wants to buy. But fire curls in my gut at the thought of my girl going without and Nichole knows how to play this card well.

I'll call you tonight. I have an appointment.

I need the money NOW.

Jesus *Christ.*

I shove my phone in my pocket and stalk into the building when the doorman holds the door for me. When I enter the lobby, I call Myers.

"Hey, man. I'm here."

"Perfect. Thanks for pinch hitting."

"Yeah. Didn't do this out of the kindness of my heart, man."

He huffs out a laugh on the other end of the phone. "I get you. Ok, so you know you're going up to the twelfth floor." I nod and punch the number. "Yep."

"When you get there, Tamara will let you into your office. I've already left her instructions. There's an intake form on the iPad, and I want you to record your entire conversation with our client. The office is totally secured and soundproof, so you have privacy, but use the app I have listed on the intake form to record her so we don't miss anything. Name's Mary Webster."

"Got it." Seems straightforward enough. I didn't know I had an office.

"Then after you meet with her and get her story, you tell her I'll be in touch this afternoon. Okay?"

"Yep."

I disconnect the call as I get to the twelfth floor and the glass doors to the elevator slide open. The only person here is a young woman with thick black hair tucked into a bun at the nape of her neck. She's got to be barely out of college, but she looks serious and staid, round glasses perched on her nose. She's wearing a white, button-down blouse, and when she sees me, her eyes go wide, and she gets to her feet.

"Mr. Cannon?"

I extend my hand. "Call me Brax. Tamara?"

She smiles, revealing perfectly white teeth, craning her neck up to see me. I'm a big guy, and easily a foot taller than she is. "Yes, sir. Follow me, please. Your client already arrived and our space here is limited, so I've seated her. You spoke to Stefan?"

"Yep."

She slides from behind the desk, and gestures for me to follow her down the hall. This place is small and clean, carpeted in beige, devoid of any decorations.

I'd been working on Stefan's cars in my body shop for over ten years, and we became friends. I trust him and know that this business he's got is thriving.

Jesus. Talk about being thrown to the wolves. I have literally no idea what I'm doing yet, and I'm already meeting with a client. For a brief minute, I wish I was back at Verge. When people call me *sir* there, it feels natural and right, reminding me that I'm the man in charge, making sure everyone's playing safe. Here, it feels odd and out of place, like I'm pretending to be something I'm not.

But as a dominant, I've learned to get my shit together and keep my head on straight. Staying cool, calm, and collected is part of the job. I'm not pretending anything. I was hired to protect people. This is white collar and not as fun as the kinkier job I have protecting people, but it can't be that different. Be aware of danger and keep the innocent safe.

She opens a door, and a petite woman gets to her feet, her back to us.

"So then you should have everything you need. Please dial thirty-three on the in-office line if you need anything."

"Got it."

The door shuts and the woman turns, startled at the sound of my voice.

Christ.

I know those wide blue eyes and pinked cheeks. They were in my bed this morning.

"Brax?" Zoe is still wearing the light blue dress, though her hair is fixed and her make-up impeccable now. One hand clutches her throat, but it doesn't mask the way she swallows nervously. "What are you doing here?" Her eyes narrow and she takes a step back, hitting the desk with her ass. "Wait. Did you follow me?"

"Nice to meet you, *Mary*," I say, prowling in the room, surprise melting to anger now that she's got the nerve to accuse me of following her. What the hell is this? And who the hell is she? "Sit." I deliver the order sharply. Eyeing me, she obeys, folding herself into a chair.

"What are you doing here?" she asks, cheeks flushed. She grabs her bag and holds it so tightly between her hands her knuckles are white.

"I've been hired to do private investigative work by

Stefan Myers," I say. If she's sitting here, she's come as a client, and I have nothing to hide. "I wasn't supposed to start until later today, but something came up and they needed me." I look around the room. It's simple and clean, the same beige Berber carpet in here as the hallway, a plain mahogany desk with a phone, a computer, and a few other devices I'm not yet familiar with, pens and paper, and a large, black leather swivel chair. I take the seat, lean back, and clasp my fingers together. "I think it's time you tell me who you are and why you're here. What's the truth? Zoe or Mary?"

She swallows and looks away but doesn't answer at first, her lips adorably pouty when pursed like she's got them now. I remember what those lips tasted like. I remember how they parted when I pulled her head back and made her moan. She was as pliant as putty then. She doesn't answer.

"My name is Braxton Cannon," I say, keeping my eyes trained on hers. "Now tell me your name, please." Though I ask her politely, my tone brooks no argument.

She blinks, swallows, then lifts her head high. The phone rings just before she speaks, and she winces, reminding me that the girl's hungover. I feel a pang of remorse, but I can't help her if she isn't honest with me.

"Zoe," she says. "My real name is Zoe." She juts her chin upward in defiance. "You can ask Beatrice if you don't believe me."

I nod. "So you gave a fake name to a private investigation company? How does that make sense?"

Her eyes narrow and she sits up straighter in her chair. "Only on the phone, *Mr.* Cannon."

I remember then that this room is soundproof, and Stefan says no one can hear anything until I record. I push my chair up to the desk, lean in, and give her the full effect of my glare. God, how I want to teach her manners with the palm of my hand against her ass.

"Drop the attitude, Zoe," I order. "You raced out of my bed this morning to this meeting which, as luck would have it, happens to be with me. I'm here to do your intake and report back to Myers. This isn't the time to stonewall me. Yeah, we spent the night together. Now we move on." I try to ignore the way she flinches when I say that, but I feel it straight to my heart. "But now, I have a job to do." I lean forward and get her full attention. "And the only way we move on is with full transparency."

She swallows hard and wipes her hands nervously on her knees. "Okay." She nods. "Yeah. Okay, alright."

The irritation I felt now wanes. She's here because she needs help, and hell if I don't want to help her. "Your real name is Zoe."

"*Yes*," she says with vehemence, as if pleading with me to listen, and just that quickly, the anger fades and I realize how vulnerable she looks now. There are circles under her eyes that tell me she's not sleeping well. "I'm not lying, Brax. I'm here to get help and I had every intention of telling the people I hired my real name." She takes a breath, then exhales it slowly. "As I said, I just didn't want my name on record."

That makes sense. I lean back in my chair and eye her. I believe her. She breathes in deep, her chest rising, then her shoulders slouching before she continues. "I had no idea you worked with Myers."

"Until this morning, neither did I."

She laughs, a pretty, musical giggle that pokes fun of the whole thing. Then I remember my gripe with her.

"Why didn't you call me when you got home?" I fix her with a stern look that makes her squirm in her chair, but her gaze doesn't waver.

"You told me to call you when I got home," she reminds me, her voice dropping to a husky, low tone. She swallows. "And I haven't been home yet." *Fuck*. I'm getting hard just thinking about her being with me last night. She was so damn responsive, it was gorgeous. She clears her throat, and I realize I'm leaning closer to her, as if my body needs to feel her heat, breathe her air.

I blink. I need to get it together.

I pull up the iPad and lay it on the table. "Okay, Zoe. I'm going to hit this button and we're gonna record what you need to say. Myers' orders."

She shakes her head wildly, beautiful eyes wide and fearful. Her hand clutches her throat. "I can't do that," she whispers, and her eyes flutter closed. She takes a huge breath, and her hands begin to shake. I watch in surprise as she flushes pink and shakes her head. "I can't. No way can you record anything." She gets to her feet, wobbly and scared and heads to the door. "This was a mistake," she gasps, and heads for the door.

Oh hell *no*.

I push back from my chair, and in two long strides I pass her, blocking her exit. Her jaw clenches and she tries to push past me, but I take her wrist between my thumb and forefinger, holding her tight. Her nostrils flare, but before she can speak, I do. "Go sit back down, Zoe," I tell her. She stares at me but is frozen with her wrist held in my hand, unsure of what to do. I gentle my voice, since it's fear that's causing her to act defiantly. I remind myself that this is my job, and she's not my sub, but hell if I don't automatically slip into my dominant headspace. I can't help it any more than a father could stop himself from being paternal. This part of me flows through my veins, my purpose clear, underscoring my conviction to help her.

I wanted her last night before I even knew she was in danger. Now? I don't want to let her out of my sight.

She still doesn't waver, though. I gentle my voice. "Zoe, you're safe here. Please. Go sit down." Though I ask her softly, I'm applying gentle pressure to her and leading her back to the chair. With a sigh, she walks back to the chair and then folds herself in it gracefully, eyes never leaving me.

I wait until it looks like she's not going to leave before I take my position behind my desk.

"Alright. Now tell me why you're here."

She swallows. "I dated a police officer," she begins. "He and I were... close." Her eyes don't leave mine, and I try to hide any reaction to what she's telling me. I hardly even know her, and I don't want to hear about whoever she was with before.

I nod, encouraging her.

"I was in grad school at the Academy."

She swallows, then continues. "And we got to know each other. I... well, we started dating," she says, her eyes looking away from me. I wonder how much she remembers from last night. Clearly, something. "We dated for a little while," she said. "I mean, I'd somehow managed to convince myself he was *The. One.* But... something was off. Something wasn't right. He didn't do things I thought, like, a *cop* would. I mean, he had the uniform and handcuffs and the badge. But he did... concerning things."

My eyes quickly look at the recording. It's going, and I don't want her to focus on that, so I shift my body closer to hers. Right now, I have to listen and not act. Is she just a girl who's overreacting? Is she the type who's overdramatic and sees ghosts where there are none? Or does she have a legitimate complaint here?

"Okay, Zoe. Details. What kinds of things did he do that concerned you?"

"Jesus," she whispers, pointing to the recorder. She frowns and makes a slashing sign with her fingers. I look at her quizzically, but she pulls out her phone and rapidly types something. She hands me the phone and points a finger at the text screen.

Shut the fucking recorder off and I'll tell you everything.

My gaze wanders from the recording to Zoe. Her voice rises, and she speaks loud and clear. "I am not sure I'm comfortable sharing anything else, Mr. Cannon."

I weigh my options, then with a shrug, I put hit the *off* button on the recording.

"Alright, Zoe. Now it's time you tell me the truth."

Chapter 4

Zoe

I don't know what it is about that recording. I shouldn't trust Brax. I mean, I just met the guy. But somehow, already, I'm feeling that I can trust him more than these men I've hired to be my private investigators. I obviously didn't know Brax worked for them when I hired them. And Jesus, I need to get everything off my chest. I need to tell *someone*. I can't stand this anymore, holding everything in. I didn't go home last night because I was with Brax, but that was only part of the reason. Ben Hoffman's onto me, and I don't feel safe unless I'm surrounded by a crowd of people.

It all comes tumbling back when I'm sober.

I know too much.

Brax is looking at me across the table as if he isn't quite sure what he's going to do with me. I have to tell him everything. Jesus, I have to tell *someone*.

"Are you sure we're safe here?" I ask him. "Seriously, I just…" I shake my head.

"Hold my hand." His low, even tone sends a shiver down my spine. Without conscious thought, I reach out and place my hand in his. I don't realize it's shaking until both of his larger, warmer hands envelop mine, the warmth seeping through my skin. I don't know if it's because we shared a night together, or there's something about Brax that makes me feel safe, but in that moment, I don't want to just tell him why I'm here, like he's some sort of confessor. I want to give it all to him, and not just what's threatening me now. *Everything*.

The upbringing I had being passed from one foster home to the next. The abuse I suffered under the hands of the people who were supposed to be my protectors. The way I drank myself into oblivion and lost my virginity to the linebacker on my college football team, and the awful, painful, tragic way that ended. I close my eyes briefly. I can still remember the positive pregnancy test, followed by excruciating pain when I lost the baby the following month. No amount of alcohol blocks out shit like that.

"Hey." His voice sounds distanced, as if he's speaking to me through a tunnel, and I realize I zoned out there. His hands tighten on mine. "Zoe." His deep voice almost startles me. I blink, looking up at him. Those eyes that danced with laughter and lust the night before now look on me with a tenderness that's almost too painful to bear.

I don't want his pity.

The pulse on my wrist taps against his hand.

"You ready to talk?" he asks.

I nod and swallow. I'm strong. I'm capable. I dug myself out of misery and rose to where I am now. I won't cave when I need to stay strong.

And I need to tell someone.

"I dated an officer, Ben Hoffman, when I was taking a grad school at the Academy a few months ago," I explain. My voice strengthens as I continue. "We really shouldn't have been together. It's really frowned about to date at the

Academy. Anyway, I suspected things were off with him from the beginning, but I ignored my gut instincts. He was extravagant, pretty pushy, and very secretive. I ignored all those things, though. But one night, things happened that made me realize he was into things he shouldn't have been."

Brax watches me calmly from below dark, serious brows. "Go on."

"He was taking a shower. He always put his phone away, but I was really sleepy, and I reached for his phone instead of mine. I saw a text come in, and it confused me, because I didn't realize what it meant at first. I didn't realize that I was never meant to see it."

He nods encouragingly but remains silent.

"It said 'The money's been wired. Zandetti needs to be dealt with. Eliminate him.' I read it over and over until the sound of the water in the shower stopped, and then I placed the phone back and pretended I was sleeping." I swallow. "Zandetti was the name of my political science professor in college. And I know in NYC there are so many people, that it's often only coincidence when people have the same name. But there was something wrong about this. And then all the little things that had set me on alert before started to look very, very different."

He nods. "Go on."

I take in a deep, shaky breath, then continue. "Hoffman would never allow me to meet him on campus. He always had to meet me at work, and he would have these conversations on the phone that I was never allowed to hear. I just assumed he was a private guy, but that night my suspicion grew. He came out of the shower, and I pretended I was asleep, but then he reached for his phone and mumbled something to himself and swore. A few minutes later he shook me awake to tell me a friend of his was in trouble and needed him and told me to get some rest before I left for class the next day. He left." I swallow, as my imagination plays out what could have happened over and over again. "The next day, my professor didn't show up for class. Eventually, word got spread around campus that he was missing." I sigh, my voice dropping as I remember. "I stayed with Hoffman. I was afraid if I broke up with him in the middle of all this, he'd know I suspected something." My voice grows shaky. "About one week later, Professor Zandetti was found dead, his body was found in Central Park Lake."

"Jesus."

"Hoffman never knew I knew anything, or so I thought. But things got weird after that, and I disliked it. I never knew for sure what was happening. I went on to do some digging of my own."

Brax lets out a low, guttural sound of disapproval but says nothing.

"Hoffman has affiliations everywhere. Political ties. He covered his tracks well, but I knew he was into illicit activities. I broke it off with him, when I felt I couldn't trust him anymore. I'm certain he never knew I suspected a thing."

"You can't be certain of anything," he says, his voice low but controlled. He still holds my hand, but now his thumb is gently circling, while he thinks. "Are you still in touch with Hoffman?"

I shake my head. "No. We broke it off about two months ago, but recently things in my place have been missing, and I feel like someone's following me, and it's become really clear to me he has friends in high places. I can't go to the police with this. Hell, I *am* the police and Hoffman's connections run deep. So," I shrug. "I came here."

He nods. "You came to the right place. I need to process this and give it to Myers, though."

I take in a deep breath. "What if I don't want it to go that way, though? Why can't you take me on alone?"

"Me?" he asks. With a sigh, he shrugs. "I'm here because they need the raw muscle. I can investigate Hoffman and see if there are any connections, but you came here because you need a team to help you."

I frown. I like being with *him*, not the other guys. Even though I've never even met the other people he works with, I already know this is what I want. He nods slowly.

"Tell you what. You never need to communicate with anyone else. I'll relay information but use their skills where mine are lacking. And I'll brief you whenever we need to make a move. Understood?"

"Yes," I say. That I can get behind. I think.

To my surprise, he lifts my hand to his mouth and gently places a kiss atop. "I won't let anyone hurt you, Zoe. But I can't change who I am. I'm the guy who's going to protect your ass, no matter what goes down. The only way this will work is if you let me, though."

Well now that's sort of a weird thing to say. "Why would I stop you?"

He raises a brow and cocks his head to the side. "I don't want you be put yourself in danger," he says. "So if I tell you to do something, I expect you follow through. Do you get me?"

"Well, sure. Yeah. That's why I'm here."

His shoulders shake with a rumble that I don't recognize at first as laughter. "We'll see about that," he says. "So first, I want you to take me back to your place. I want to be sure it's safe, and I want to know the location. Okay?"

I'm pretty sure this goes above and beyond the whole private investigator thing.

"Okay, listen," I tell him. "I'm not some damsel in distress, okay? I'm a trained officer, and I don't need your protection. I didn't come here for that. I came here because I need to find out what's going on, and I need more than I'm capable of doing on my own."

I get angry, then, feeling my chest rising with the effort of keeping myself unruffled.

"And you will," he says with maddening calm. "But not without having some rules in place."

Rules? What the hell is he talking about? No *way*.

"Are you fucking high?" I ask him. "I said I don't *need* a keeper." I roll my eyes and push away from the desk. This was a mistake. I've been in law enforcement long enough that I know going to any of my superiors or anyone else on the force would end in disaster. Why the hell am I here? What am I doing with myself?

"Zoe," he warns, standing up and pushing the chair behind him as he rises.

"Seriously, Braxton, I'm fine. I shouldn't have come here," I say, and I turn to leave. He walks beside me but says nothing, just takes long, purposeful strides keeping up with mine, pushing his way to the door. With one shove, the door swings open. The secretary in the front gets to her feet, startled, and looks at us with wide eyes.

"Do you need anything Mr. Cannon?" she asks, tilting her head to the side. For some reason, that pisses me off. Seriously, why does she have to bend over backward like that to please him?

I frown, and march past her, but he follows by my side. "All set for now," he says to the secretary. "We'll talk later. I'll make sure I fill in Myers. Thank you."

He opens the door to the exit, waits for me, and I go through. The bright sky nearly blinds me, and I halt, putting my hand to my eyes to shield them.

"I'll see you home," he says.

"Seriously, I'm fine," I say, but he takes my hand then hails down a taxi.

"I didn't ask," he says, as he blows out an angry breath. "Jesus, you need your ass spanked."

"You need your balls kicked," I mutter in a knee-jerk reaction that surprises me.

He doesn't respond, but his eyes narrow and the grip on my hand tightens.

I kinda like that he's coming with me, but don't really want him to know how I feel about this.

He gestures for me to get into the taxi, and right then I feel something totally different than I have before. No one ever looks out for me like this. I'm the one in charge, the one with the power, but his deferential treatment of me is unusual and, if I admit it, a little sweet. A *little*.

I won't let him know that though. I slide into the musty-smelling taxi and he follows suit, his huge frame taking up so much of the seat it's almost comical as our knees knock into each other. The door shuts, and the taxi driver turns to us. "Where to?"

"758 Park Terrace, the Gild," I instruct. "The Gild" is short for "Gild Apartment Buildings," where my apartment lies several miles away, the little oasis I've built for myself that I've spent literally years creating. This is where I need to be. I'm suddenly totally aware that I didn't sleep in my bed last night. I want to. I want to be alone, in my own bed. But as the taxi takes a turn, my knees bang into his, and I turn to move away but his large, massive hand sprawls over my knee and steadies the trembling.

"The Gild?" he asks.

I nod. They're a little on the high-end side, but this is what I need. Spending years going from one home to the next does something to a girl. I never wanted anything more in my life as badly as I wanted a quiet place of my own.

We drive in silence, and I focus on keeping my breathing steady. I can't calm the fuck down if I'm letting my head spiral out of control. Somehow, having him here with me like this, and the visit to the agency is a little too much for me. Overwhelming. Somehow, this situation is far more real now that he's sitting next to me, as if his very presence makes the danger that lurks in the shadows far more real. This reminds me of our night together, how he held me close. How he kissed me tenderly and rough, then fucked me so perfectly I climaxed with his name on my lips. I remember the feel of his huge, dominant, warm hands on my thighs, on my breasts, cupping my ass. And I can't help but wonder what else we could've done.

We were at a BDSM Club. There were people half-dressed who were doing all sorts of things I had no idea about, and they were *liking* it. Why am I pushing away the one man who had the balls to take me on in freaking *ever?* Maybe this *can* work.

The man identifies as a dom. Is that why Bea didn't want me to leave with him? Does that mean Zack is a dom or something, too? Why wouldn't he tell me? We're hardly superficial people, but there's something to be said for needing some privacy. Part of the downside of being on the force means that your life is not your own.

The cab pulls up in front of my apartment building, and Brax gets out first, after handing a wad of cash to the driver. Frowning, I yank the money out of the man's hand and slip my own in. Brax doesn't see it because he's already out of the car. "Thanks," I say to the driver, ignoring Brax's hand as it's held out to me. I get up and move past him and as the taxi pulls away, I hand him his money back.

"I can take care of myself," I insist. He eyes the cash

with a frown, but says nothing, just shoves it in his pocket. "I don't think that following me to my apartment was part of our agreement," I remind him. "In fact, if I remember correctly, we don't *have* an agreement and we never have."

"You know what..." Brax says.

"What?" I snap.

"Do you think you can stop being bitchy for a minute and listen to me, instead of making your mind up about me before you ever even have the time to form an honest opinion?"

Bitchy? Jesus. Who the hell does he think he is?

He takes me by the hand and leads me into my building.

"I'm not being a *bitch*, Braxton," I protest. "*God.*"

"I didn't say you were a bitch," he says. "I said you were *being bitchy.* There's a difference."

Dude. Hardly.

I roll my eyes and lead him to my apartment.

"God," he mutters. "Like I said. You need a good spanking."

"Hey!"

"What?"

We're at my apartment now, and I wish my body didn't respond to him so powerfully. At the word *spanking*, and the memory of what happened the night before, my heart flutters in my chest. Jesus, he's hot, all big and strong and growly like this, even if I do want to sorta push him down the stairs. I eye him with curiosity when we reach the third floor and I open the door to my apartment. If push comes to shove, I could probably take him. I've been trained in self-defense, and I bet I could handle him just fine.

The door swings open to my apartment and I gesture for him to follow me, but before I can get a word out, I see a dark blur out of the corner of my eye, like there's some sort of meteor or comet falling from the sky, but in a moment, I realize it isn't anything like that at all, but a man, screaming with maddening vehemence as he charges toward us. This is total bullshit.

Instinctively, I assume the fighting stance, feet spread, and my knees bent slightly, ready to protect myself. My assailant swings a fist straight at me, but I duck, then block a second blow, pivot, and grab the arm that was swinging to attack me. With a rapid tug, I bring both of us to the ground, but I've got the upper hand now. I take him by the back of the head and slam his face into the ground, blood spurting from his nose in crimson rivulets. Now that he's pinned to the ground, I hold his wrists in my hand. Fuck, I don't have my cuffs or any weapons on me.

"I need you to keep him down while I make some calls," I say to Brax, but that second of lost attention on the guy beneath me is my downfall. He shoves up so fast from the floor I lose my balance. Brax reaches to help but the man slashes out, his hand fisting a knife that almost slices through Brax, but he dodges just in time. I lunge for him, but he's too fast, and before I know what's happening, the door to my apartment is swinging open and the son of a bitch is escaping. I run, needing to catch him, but Brax's deep, booming voice halts me in my place.

"Zoe, *no!*"

I'm startled too much to act and by the time I realize I'm listening to Brax and not meaning to, my lead on the guy is gone. I growl in rage, furious he stopped me, and nearly shake my fist at him in a fit of temper as I race into the hallway. It's too late. The guy's gone.

I storm back into my apartment and glare at Brax.

"Why'd you do that?" I snap, marching over to him and without conscious thought, shoving my hands on his chest so he reels backward and his lower back smacks into the counter in my kitchen. I feel a pang of guilt as he stumbles but I immediately suppress it. I want to beat the shit out of the guy. I advance on him before he has a chance to fully recover and swing my fist out to deck him. God, he's got me so mad I can hardly see straight, blood pounding in my ears, my head light with heat and anger but my purpose clear. I want him to know he doesn't pull this with me. But as I swing, he ducks my blow, then dives, arms straight out so he grabs me around the torso and wrestles me straight to the floor.

I'm flat on my back and he's above me, one knee on either side of me, his massive hands pinning my wrists by my side. I try to flail but can't, naturally, pinned like this. I may be trained, but even training doesn't move a mountain off your chest.

"You *asshole,*" I grit out, trying to push him to no avail. "I needed to see who the fuck that was and you had the nerve to stop me? What did you think you were doing?"

His nostrils flare, his eyes flashing at me, and I can tell he's restraining himself. "You have no idea how many people he was with, who's still fucking out there. Who could be *in here.*"

"What? There was a break-in. God! Some jerk was trying to steal my shit, and he didn't expect to have some blowback to that. You're acting like I was just ambushed or something."

He rolls his eyes heavenward, but his grip on me doesn't diminish. "You think this was an isolated incident? Jesus, Zoe. Get your head outta your ass."

I squirm and try one more time to push him off me, but he only looks mildly amused and doesn't budge. He continues. "You come to a private investigator for help, and magically an assailant appears in your apartment. And you don't think the two are related?"

Of course I think the two are related, but I don't want to give him the satisfaction of being right.

"I'm gonna go check this place to make sure it's clear, and you're gonna stay right here and not move a muscle." He glares me into submission. "Do you understand me?"

"Fine," I spit out, just wanting to sit up and rub my wrists.

He watches me for a full minute before he lets go of my wrists and stalks past my kitchen and through my apartment. I hear doors opening and closing.

Someone could be in my closet. I close my eyes briefly. To my utter shock and disgust, my throat is tight, and my nose is tingly. And just that easily, I'm that kid again, hiding in a closet to save her ass. I know what it's like to be hurt by someone who could beat you just because they were bigger. I know what it's like to fear the sound of a door opening and wonder if tonight is the night he'd come home drunk and take out his anger and self-loathing on me. I made up my mind the day I broke free that I'd never let someone attack me again without a fight.

But Jesus, the anger burns in me like a furnace, steady, scorching, like embers in a bonfire, ready to ignite. And when I suppress my anger, it comes out in my emotions. If I cry now, I'll never be able to look at him again.

Who was I last night? Why'd I ever let go of the control I cling so tightly to and let this guy fuck me? Now he thinks he's some sort of boss of me. Who *does* that?

I sit up and rub my wrists when he comes back in. "Coast is clear."

And then he does the unthinkable. His voice softens as he kneels beside me, and he's talking in a low, soothing tone instead of one riddled with anger. "Listen, Zoe. Can we talk calmly? Or do I need to tie you up?"

I glare at him, not moving, trying to quickly assess the

situation so I can take him down if necessary, but I hesitate too long. He bends down and takes both my wrists in hand, pinning them by my side. "Do I?" he repeats, his fingers flexing on my flesh.

He's not joking. His eyes meet mine in bold challenge. I stare at him, not sure how to respond at first, and then a corner of his lips quirks up. "It's sort of my specialty, you know."

I blink. "What?"

"Bondage."

I huff out a breath. "Leave it to you to make this whole thing sexual. Jesus. Sleep with a guy once and now I have to put up with the jokes forever?"

His eyes narrow. "Yeah, I'm not joking."

I don't know if it's because he fucked me senseless the night before, or because I'm still buzzing from the ridiculous amount of alcohol I consumed or what, but my mind immediately begins playing tricks on me. I imagine myself in the room where we were the night before, but now I'm tied up, his ropes around my wrists, crisscrossed around my body. A part of me wants to feel that. To experience that level of trust. To relinquish all control.

"Oh yeah?" I ask, my voice lower and husky. Maybe if I pretend to be overpowered he'll let me go. "You're the bondage king?"

He lifts one shoulder in a half-shrug, as if pretending to be modest. "Something like that." He sobers. "Now answer the question."

"Fine."

I'm not sure if I've managed to convince him or to trick him into believing that it's that easy to subdue me, but finally he gives an almost imperceptible nod, and he lets go of my wrists before he slides off me to the side. I wait until I have my bearings, then I shove him the rest of the way off me, taking advantage of his momentary shock before he springs into action. I wriggle out from beneath him, pivot and lunge. I've done this so many times I could do it in my sleep, besting a man twice my size by being lithe and fast, and all I need to do is pin him down beneath me to make my point. My heart surges with pride now that he's pinned beneath me, and there's nothing but grunts and curse words in the kitchen as I make sure to subdue him without smashing his head on the tiled floor. Then he twists, heaves, and now I find myself sprawling.

Shit.

I scramble but it's no use. I can't get my bearings, can't get away.

"You asshole," I grind out, but his hands are on me now, firmer than before.

"Can't believe you just played me for a fool," I hear him. He looks at me once, shakes his head, then flips me so I'm belly down on the floor and he's behind me, and he's got the upper hand again.

There comes a point in any combat scenario where you know you're losing. You know your only chance of overcoming your opponent is gone. In a staged scenario, like the training sessions at the academy, you might get hit a few times but admitting defeat will usually end the session, unless you're at the mercy of an asshole who has a bone to pick with you. In a real-life situation, you know you're going down. It's rare that someone will actually take a fight to the death. Even the most hardened criminals often have trouble pulling the trigger, finishing the job. Most of the time it just means you're getting a beating.

Fuck it.

I have no idea what Brax will do. All I know is he restrained me once and that didn't end up so well for him, so the likelihood of him upping his game is pretty damn strong. He's gonna win this one. There's no denying that, but I'm not going down without a fight.

I struggle and try to push away, but I find that he's taking a weird position. He's like kneeling or something instead of trying to pin me down again. He lifts me straight up in the air like I'm a rag doll and hauls me straight across his knees. It takes me a second to register the position I'm in before his palm smacks against my ass. I don't even react at first, I'm so shocked at what he's doing.

I've been wrestled and beaten and subdued. But hell. This is different.

"What the fuck!" I protest, as a second vicious smack of his palm on my ass pushes the breath right out of me. "What the hell are you doing?"

He doesn't say anything. He just sorta shifts his position so that now my head is lower on the floor and my ass is higher up in the air, giving him what I'd imagine is a very clear target.

"Brax!"

In silence, he pins me down and gives me two, three, four wicked spanks.

This feels weird. I'm not sure what to do. It hurts, I can't deny it, and I would have expected I'd feel like a kid or something, being spanked like this. He spanks me again, and again, and I can't even fight him now. I've tried that, and it got me nowhere. I've got to try another tactic.

"I'm sorry!" I manage to squeak out in between whacks of his brutal palm. "Ok, I'm sorry!"

He pauses and rests his hand on my scorched ass. He's heaving with the effort of restraining and spanking me, and for a moment the only sound in the kitchen is both of us panting.

"Seriously. I'm sorry. I shouldn't have done that," I say. Weirdly, the desire to beat him has fled, and I have to admit I'm actually feeling pretty subdued. What the hell happened there? "Please let me up and we can talk."

To my surprise, I feel his hand fisting my hair at the nape of my neck, it's all tangled up in his fingers. He pulls my head back and his mouth is at my ear. Warm breath tickles my skin, but it's what he says that makes me tingle. "You ever fucking pull something like that again, I'll bare your ass before I spank you. You understand me?"

"Yes," I agree, just needing him to release me now. But he doesn't, not yet. He lets go of his grip in my hair, but still holds me firmly over his lap. Now his hand rests on my scorched skin, and he's speaking calmly, as if he's in complete control. I'm not sure what he's doing, but then I realize he's rubbing out the sting on my ass.

"You sure you're gonna behave now?"

I swallow and nod. The feel of his hand on my ass is turning me the hell on, but I don't want him to know that. Now that things are calm, and he isn't spanking my ass any longer, a part of me has to admit… even though he's a jerk, that was really fucking hot. Just like the night before when he went all dom on me, I find myself needing to be taken to another place. My skin's on fire, and I feel a low pulse of arousal between my legs as he continues to massage my ass while talking to me in low, soothing tones.

"Swear to God, I've never spanked a woman like that before," he says. "I've only ever done it when we agree at the club." He pauses, and there's either humor or anger in his voice when he speaks again. Maybe both. "You deserved it, though."

"I'm not sure if there's such a thing as any grown, mature woman who deserves a spanking, Braxton," I say, attempting to hold onto a shred of my dignity.

He releases me and pulls me up so I'm sitting on his lap. Leaning back, he's now got his back to the wall as he pulls me tight against his chest. "We're gonna have to agree to disagree on that point." Despite my earlier anger, I'm feeling like a subdued little kitten with a bellyful of milk now. He's right there, strong and stern and reassuring. "And answer the question honestly," he says, one massive hand reaching out to cup my cheek. "You aren't turned on at all?"

Damn him and his clairvoyant ways. Without waiting for a response, his hand moves from my jaw to my neck, he tips my head back, and he kisses my neck. I shiver when his lips touch the sensitive skin. His tongue flicks out and traces a path along the sensitive skin. "Not even a little?"

Of course I'm turned on. Who wouldn't be after that?

"Maybe a little," I whisper but my voice trails off to a groan as his teeth sink into my neck before he kisses there once again.

He pulls away, removing his hands and his mouth, and gets to his feet. "We need to get out of here," he says.

I'm still momentarily stunned by the kiss, but then I realize, as if waking up from a dream, that my arm is sore, and my torso is bruised, and we're still sprawled on my kitchen floor. I scramble to my feet as he does.

"Pack a bag," he says. "I'm taking you to Verge. It's the safest place we can go, with 24/7 surveillance and close to Myers. I can be in touch with him, and we can track down whoever the fuck is on your tail."

Leave my apartment?

"Why the fuck would I do that?" I ask, frowning at him. "I can defend myself."

He's halfway across the tiny dining area when he turns, frowning. "You can defend yourself," he says, and he's actually agreeing, not contradicting me. "Clearly. But this isn't just about defending yourself. As much as I hate the idea of you being alone in this place and maybe *more* than one of them coming after you, let's put two and two together here. They obviously know where you live, yeah. But did you or did you not come to me because you want to find out who's after you and how we bring them down?"

He turns and crosses his arms on his chest, biceps bulging as he fixes me with a stern glare.

God, I hate this feeling of helplessness.

I swallow. "I did. But I don't want to give up my privacy." Or my independence or autonomy. Jesus, I fought tooth and nail for this and it didn't come easy.

He works his jaw, staring at me for a moment, then shrugs. "I didn't say you had to give up your privacy. I'll get you a private room and we'll make sure you're under an assumed name temporarily. It won't be for long."

How does he know that?

"I'm not sure why your club is any safer than my apartment," I protest, even though I do know. My place is a rental, as is the case with most homes in NYC, and I've barely outfitted it with safety locks. He raises his brows and looks at the enormous sliding glass doors that lead to my balcony.

"Second floor balcony, with..." his voice trails off as he walks over shaking his head, fingering the flimsy lock, "a lock that doesn't look like it can keep a toddler out?" Then he walks over to the entryway door. "You have *one lock* on this door. No deadbolt." He leans back against the door, his eyes roaming heavenward as if he's contemplating something, and he ticks off his points on his fingers as he continues. "Verge has *one* main entrance, not including the emergency exits which are, as you might guess, alarmed, and only used in case of emergency and never for entry to the club. There's at least one trained bouncer at the door every night, and many times, that bouncer is *me*. Once we get past the main entrance, the only people allowed in are vetted, with the exception of guests who are there by invitation only. People mingle on the main floors, except in the private rooms, which are only occupied by long-term members. Zack Williams, who as you know is an NYPD detective and fully trained in all manner of defense, comes frequently. You've got a fucking barricade of men *and* women ready to take down assailants at a moment's notice, and as I said before, a short distance away you have Myers and his men." He pauses. "*You* don't even have a dog."

"I don't need your protection," I protest. I can handle myself, and I half expect him to railroad me and toss me over his shoulder like he did the first night we met. Though I have to admit the idea of being manhandled is theoretically hot, and a small, teensy little part of me sorta wishes he'd do it again, I'm serious. I truly don't want to give up my freedom and hand it all to him. I've never needed a man to protect me and I don't need one now.

Men have only ever fucked me over. Although Brax seems nice and all, I don't know him well enough to know if he's different. I respect that some women like being protected by the big, strong, manly man or whatever the fuck. But that isn't me.

I didn't join the police force only to surrender myself to someone with a dick.

My heartbeat is ratcheting up as I wonder if he'll react, and my ass still tingles from the spanking he gave me in the kitchen. I swallow, wondering how he'll respond, and how hard I need to push this issue. Even though I don't want someone to protect me, I have to admit I'm not thrilled about staying here alone right now.

"I didn't say you need my protection," he says with infuriating calm. "What I'm doing is offering you a safer place to stay while we figure shit out."

Huh.

He continues. "You wear a seat belt when you're driving?"

"Yeah, of course."

"You wear protective gear when you're at the shooting range?"

"Yes," I say warily.

"You ever take safety precautions when you're responding to a call."

"Yes," I say, getting angry now, my voice tight. "God, I get your point."

"You don't do any of that shit because you're expecting danger to happen, or because you can't handle it if you do. You do that as safety precautions. Something to make sure that if anything goes wrong, you don't end up caught with your pants down."

A nervous giggle bubbles up and I barely suppress it, letting out a little huff of a laugh. It's a super common expression, *caught with your pants down*, one my supervisor favors, and I've heard a million times, but somehow hearing Brax say it makes the reality of my situation so much more real. He, however, doesn't seem amused at all.

"You gonna do what I say, or do I need to call Zack?"

Wait. What? "Brax, we're not getting Zack in on this. No way. Are you out of your mind?"

His eyes narrow. "I'm about done with you questioning my sanity." The stern tone of his voice makes my tummy flutter a little. I like it when he goes all serious and dom on me. Hell, my panties are damp from what just happened in the kitchen.

Oh, God. What the hell is he doing to me?

He inhales, squares his shoulders, and places both hands on his hips.

"I trust Zack with my life," he says.

"Yeah," I say, turning away. I do, too. But somehow,

changing the way things are—telling Zack about what's going on, moving temporarily to Verge, even hiring these P.I. guys, feels more dangerous. But why did I go to them in the first place? Really, what was I hoping to accomplish? I take in a deep breath and let it out slowly, then close my eyes as I process through everything.

I know information that could get me killed. It's not an exaggeration or dramatized in any way. I hate drama. *But this is reality.*

I went to Myers because I'd heard Zack mention Myers as head of one of the best private investigation team he'd known, even though they worked outside of law enforcement.

I had to go *outside* of law enforcement since there was no doubt in my mind that there was corruption in the very place I worked, where my friends were, where I'd put my trust.

Today, I was attacked in the safety of my own home, and the asshole who attacked me still roams free.

I'm one person against… how many?

I take in a deep breath and open my eyes. "You're right," I say with a sigh. "This is beyond my power and I came for help because I need it." It pains me to admit that. "I'll go with you to Verge. But *only* temporarily."

He gives one quick, short nod. "Good," he says. "Pack your bags and I'll call Zack." He gives me a once over, pushes away from the door, and walks over to me. When he reaches me, his eyes gentle and he tucks a stray lock of hair behind my ear, the tender gesture making me melt just a little. "You're not weak to take precautions, Zoe. Do you understand that?"

"Of course I do," I lie. No. No, I don't understand that. I want to protect myself. I want to protect others. I wouldn't have joined the NYPD otherwise. I'm fueled with a burning need to put assholes who hurt other people behind bars, to see justice served, to guard those who can't protect themselves. I go to bed every night after a long shift knowing I did my duty, that I made the world a better place for just one day. It seems a sort of betrayal to admit I need help, but I also don't want to let my stupid pride fuck this up.

He's taller than I am, and strong. When he reaches his hand out to me, I can see the ripples of his muscles beneath his shirt, the strength in his shoulders and arms as he leans in to me. "You could kick my ass, baby," he murmurs, his lips quirking.

Oh no he doesn't. That *baby* is the beginning of my unraveling.

"I can," I say, already playing the scene out with the mere suggestion. Arm up, pivot hips, knock his arm away from me. He'd bend over, and I'd elbow him, bringing him to the floor. I don't want to hurt him, though. I don't want to fight him. Just knowing I can is good enough.

"Then let's get you out of here, so you don't have to. Because if you don't move, I will, and I see now the only way I got you over my shoulder and into Verge to begin with was because you were plastered and likely horny as hell."

"Hey!" I protest, smacking his big barrel of a chest. He nabs my wrist and firmly moves my arm down by my side.

"Am I not telling the truth?"

"Fine," I huff out. "Maybe it's true."

"Zoe," he says, his voice low and corrective, a tone I'm not familiar with. He's being patient and calm, but it seems he's had enough. "There's no need to get defensive." Is this a dom thing or something? It feels weird to be spoken to like this, and I don't really understand why I feel a low thrum of need low in my belly at his tone.

"Let's go then," I say, trying to pull away from him, but he holds me fast and with a quick tug, pulls me up against his chest. Damn, he smells good, and seeing him here like this puts me right in the mindset of the night before.

Part of me wants to forget who I am and what I need to do, to have my mind quieted for just a little while. I live in a perpetual state of defense. I guess that's what happens to a girl when the people who were supposed to protect her were the ones who hurt her most. You learn to take care of yourself. You learn never to rest, even in sleep.

He's still holding my wrists pinned to my side. I could get out of this if I wanted to. One knee to his groin and he'd be done.

But I'm not sure I want to.

"I don't want you to boss me around," I lie.

"Don't you?" he asks, a brow rising even as one of his dimples makes his appearance. I'm so close I can feel when he inhales, and the whisper of his breath graces the bare skin at my neck.

"No," I insist, though my voice is breathier now, my protest weaker.

Then his gaze hardens, and he sobers, and to my disappointment, he releases my wrists. "Need to get you out of here," he says. "I'm calling Zack. You go pack a bag. Take only the bare essentials and move. You're also taking a leave of absence from work."

"What?" I blink in shock, but he's already got his phone up to his ear. He points to the bedroom and whisks his finger as if to remind me to move my ass.

I open my mouth and his eyes narrow, then he turns his back to me.

"Arrgh!" I huff in indignant anger. Who the hell does he think he is? I'd have better luck talking to a brick wall, so in a huff of anger I turn away from him and march toward my room.

"Not the boss of me," I mutter, grabbing a duffle bag out of my closet. It's not until I'm tossing my panties in the zippered mesh portion of my bag that I realize something isn't right. I'm a tidy person and everything has a place, but the little ceramic jewelry box where I keep my meager possessions is turned over, chains and bracelets and earrings spilled all atop my dresser. My computer desk is a fucking mess, papers and pens scattered to the floor, and my computer isn't where I left it. I look to my bedroom door. He scanned this place, but didn't notice what a mess it was? Maybe he thinks I'm always a mess or something.

Fucking douchebags. For a minute I wish the asshole who attacked me would come back. I'd teach him to leave me and my place alone.

With a scream of fury, I lift the sneaker from the pile of shoes I was going to pack and whip it against the wall. A black smear of rubber mars the white wall, but my fury doesn't abate. I grab the second shoe and whip that to meet its mate, a second smear joining the first. Nothing's broken so I don't much care. I need to throw things. I want to *break* things.

"Zoe, *stop.*" Brax's deep voice bellows from the doorway. I pause, mid-throw, shoe number three still grasped in my hand.

"They touched my fucking things," I growl, but I don't throw the shoe. Now that he's here, I'm a little embarrassed. I don't really want to appear childish to him. "My computer's gone. My shit's all over the place. They were looking for something, but I don't know what the hell they want from me."

His eyes soften a little, and he prowls closer, palms outstretched.

"Anything important on that computer?"

"Of course there is." I wiped everything clean, but someone with any knowledge of computers would be able to lift things. I know better than to be careless when I contacted Myers and his company, and up until today, I've never told anyone what I know.

"Well, nothing that would implicate me," I say. "But of course, I have stuff on that computer."

"You don't back up externally?"

I cross my arms on my chest and roll my eyes. "Really?" I ask, fighting the desire to toss the shoe in my hand at *him*. "I just realized someone's stolen my shit, invaded my home, and you think now's a good time to lecture me about precautionary measures one might use with important information? *God!*"

His eyes narrow, a muscle ticking in his jaw as he eyes me in silence, as if weighing the options of his response. "Pack your bags," he says with finality. "We leave in five minutes."

And with that, he stalks out. I stare at him before I realize the time is ticking and now I have four minutes. Swearing under my breath and cursing my luck, I toss everything I think I might need in a bag. I have no choice. I'll follow him to Verge. I'll contact Zack. But I'm the one that'll sort this out.

Chapter 5

Zack's on his way while Zoe finishes packing.

If she were a guy, I'd say she has cast-iron balls. Nerves of steel. I can't believe Zoe's tenacity, and if I'm honest, I have to admit, watching her take down that guy, then the way she flipped me over and pinned me down, even though she totally undermined me and was kind of a brat about it, was hot as hell. I love how she can kick ass. Some people might want a date at a restaurant or club but hell, I want to take Zoe to a shooting range. Seeing a gun in her hands, I think I'd have to fuck her up against the wall.

She's tough, and there's something deep in her eyes she's managed to hide so far with snarky comments and evasion. As a dominant, I've learned to read people, though, and I can see that there's a lot more to Zoe than meets the eye. There's fear in her eyes. I want to know why.

I'm no stranger to having shit you want buried. I fucked my life up knocking up Nichole, and even though I love Devin to pieces and would never call her a mistake, being shackled to Nichole is something I'd wish on no one.

Her dad's a preacher and he hates my guts, thinks I wrecked his girl, and her mother, some high member of society, heads up the garden club and church book club, thinks I'm part-devil or something. I don't really care what they think about me, but I'd give anything to wipe my past clean and start over.

I still remember the day her father found out I'd gotten her pregnant, the way his holier-than-thou eyes narrowed on me with barely-controlled hatred. "You were a bastard child," he said, venom in his voice. "Your mother was a whore and you're no better."

With people like him preaching the gospel and the good news of salvation, I'll take my place in line with the sinners.

My mother had me out of wedlock, yeah, and to old-fashioned people like him, that's akin to prostitution. I never knew my dad, and never will. When I was old enough to know better, I figured things out. I knew she hated what she did so we'd have food on the table, and Nichole's dad might call that prostitution but I call it survival.

You grow up, you shake that shit off and make your life your own, but you don't forget.

And I can't bury my past. Every time I pick up Devin or answer a fucking text from Nichole trying to dick around with me again, every time I have to bring Devin to her grandparents' house for holidays and look at those people, I'm that useless bastard child they scorned.

As if I've muttered some kinda incantation to conjure up my demons, my phone buzzes with a message from Nichole.

You need to come and get Devin.

I take in a deep breath and let it out slowly, while I hear Zoe fumbling around in her room.

"You almost ready?" I bark out. God, a part of me hopes this woman has kink in her blood. I need to feel control. I long to tie my ropes around her, to mete out measured, delicious pain and pleasure. I never feel more powerful than when I have a submissive quivering beneath my utter control.

"Yeah," she says. "Take a chill pill!"

I stifle a snort. Chill pill? What is this, 1997?

She's snarky as fuck and hell if that doesn't turn me on. With a frown, I reply to Nichole's message.

What the hell are you talking about? This isn't my weekend with Devin. You know I love spending time with her, but I haven't made arrangements to have her this weekend. I'm working.

I haven't even told Zoe I'm dungeon monitor tonight. I'll get her sorted back at Verge first, and then explain to her what my role is and how I'll be handling things.

Nice. What a fantastic father you are.

She baits me like I'm a fish on a line. Jesus. I decide the best action is not to respond, but a part of me can't help but wonder why she's telling me I'm taking Devin. Is she planning on taking some low-life back to her place tonight? Has she gotten back in bed with the dealer she met over the border in Canada, and now she's going to put out for him again?

The better question is: does my kid need me?

God.

I tap my foot impatiently, waiting to see if Nichole will text me again, but instead I decide to go straight to Devin. I dial Nichole's number.

"Hi," she says with guarded friendliness.

"Put Devin on the line." There's no civility between us.

"Fine. Just a minute." She loves to dick around with me, but when she wants something she's a bit more compliant.

"Daddy?"

"Hey, baby. Is everything okay?"

"Well I think so. Can I go to your place tonight?"

I swear under my breath so she doesn't hear. "Well you're always welcome with me. Can you tell me why you're asking, though? You sure everything's okay?"

There's a muffle of voices, then a door clicking shut, and I surmise Devin's left the room to speak to me privately.

"Mom told me she was going to text you to come get me. She has a date with the loser guy with the scar on his chest, and she doesn't want me around in case he wants to kiss her again. Gah-*ross.*"

Again? She's had him over before?

"Yeah. But I heard him tell her last time he doesn't like brats underfoot. He's a jerk."

I close my eyes briefly, because the anger I feel is clouding my vision. I'll give him brats underfoot, the motherfucker.

"So daddy, can I please stay with you tonight?"

I don't have to think twice. I'll figure out what to do with Zoe, and I'll get her situated. I'll have to.

"Of course, Devin. You let me know if anyone does anything they shouldn't. You hear me?"

"Yes. Pinky swear."

"Good job. I'll see you tonight, okay? Bye, honey."

I hear a door slam, and then Zoe's standing in front of me, her bag over her shoulder. She's glaring, and I fight rolling my eyes.

"Packed?" I ask.

"No," she snaps. "Decided I'd clean my closet out instead." She rolls her eyes heavenward.

"You know," I say nonchalantly, reaching for her bag, but she pulls away. "If we weren't getting the hell out of here and making sure you were safe, you and I would have a talk about a few things."

She huffs out a laugh. "Is that right?" she snaps.

I reach a second time for her bag and this time pry it out of her hands. "Give me that," I order, giving it a firm tug and ushering her out the door. "Yeah, babe. We would. I didn't do anything to deserve you giving me attitude, and in case you haven't gotten the memo, I'm not the kinda guy who puts up with brats."

She glares at me and doesn't reply at first as we make our way to the exit.

"Yeah," she says. "So who's the 'honey' you're talking to on the phone? After you kissed me this morning?" She crosses her arms on her chest and her narrowed eyes zone in on me.

Jesus. Seriously?

"My daughter."

She blinks. "Oh. I—I'll hail a cab," she says.

"Don't bother. Zack's on his way."

Her lips are pursed, her jaw clenched. To my surprise, instead of complaining, she sighs, and her voice softens. "Look, I'm sorry," she says. "I know I'm being a bitch. I just can't seem to stop myself sometimes. When I'm afraid, it comes out."

I don't expect her to apologize, so I'm not exactly sure how to respond at first, but before I can say anything, Zack pulls up curbside. I can see his light brown hair and tats from where I stand, even though the car is unfamiliar. He rolls down the window. "You rang?" He smiles, though his gaze is somewhat wary as he looks from me to Zoe. He wants to know why we're together, but he'll have to wait.

"Thanks, man," I say, putting Zoe's bag in the trunk. "Take us to Verge, and it's important you make sure we're not being followed. Got it?"

"Got it," he says. Zoe folds into the passenger seat, and I sit in the back. When the doors are shut, and the windows rolled up, he looks at both of us briefly before pulling into the road. He glances in the rearview mirrors. "No one followed me here," he says. "And I took the fastest car we own in case I need to move." He inhales then exhales slowly, driving through the busy streets with his eyes trained on the mirrors. "But I don't do this for fun, kids. You need to tell me what the fuck is going on here."

Zoe clenches her jaw and looks out the window.

"Zoe," I say warningly. I haven't known her for long at all, but I already recognize her "stonewall" face.

"I'll pull this car over," Zack says. "Honest to God, I'm not being your getaway man without knowing what the fuck's going on."

"It's not that I don't trust you," Zoe finally says, a note of desperation in her voice. "But this isn't playtime, guys. The more people that know about what's going on, the more people are in danger."

"They'll find Beatrice, Zack," she says, turning to him, her voice pleading. "I know they will." I know then it isn't about her not trusting him, but her own need to protect the people she cares about. She doesn't want Zack hurt.

He swallows hard, takes a right, and accelerates.

Why's he going so quickly?

"Someone trailing us?" God, I hate this.

"No. I just want to get to Verge." He looks briefly at Zoe before looking back at the road. "It's too late to keep me out of this," he says. "Your ass is in my car, and I'm taking you to Verge. You're in some way, and I swear to God I do *not* want details, hooked up with one of my best friends, heading to a club which you may or may not know is a kink club where Beatrice and I spend most of our free time." His jaw tightens. "So spill, Zoe."

Accepting the inevitable, she nods. "Alright then. There are people on the force involved with covering up, and even being responsible, for the death of an old professor of mine, Daniel Zandetti. From what I know, that's only the tip of the iceberg."

He nods, but his face doesn't register surprise.

She blows out a breath. "A few months ago, I was enrolled at the Academy taking a few more courses."

He nods.

"You remember how Professor Zandetti was murdered? And shortly after that, his wife went missing, and no one's seen her since?"

He nods again.

She crosses her arms on her chest, and her brows knit together. She's getting angry again, I can tell by her posture and tone. "The night before Zandetti went missing, I was with Ben Hoffman. He worked closely with Zandetti. He got a text, he was in the shower, and I read it by accident. It was a directive to take Zandetti's life. I feigned ignorance of this, and that night he went out and Zandetti went missing. His body was found in Central Park Lake."

Zack whistles softly. "I knew you wanted help from a P.I, but had no idea it involved the force. You have any more contact with Hoffman?"

"No. I broke it off with him, but even before that happened, he was always weird around me. Like he was hiding something."

Zack nods. "What do you know about Zandetti?"

"Well, he was one of the most renowned professors in the grad program, mostly known for the grants he administered totaling like five million dollars in competitive grants from the DHS."

"DHS?" I ask.

"U.S. Department of Homeland Security," she supplies.

"Got it."

"And he published in some seriously reputable paper that upheld massive reform for Homeland Security. He was a public voice of reform for illegal drug trafficking, and I suspect he made some enemies."

"Jesus. Did these people have a death wish?" I ask. Why the hell would they put themselves at risk like that?

Zoe shakes her head. "Sometimes, people get so far into intellectual headspace and the recognition they get for groundbreaking research, they negate the very real risk they take on by outing those they're after."

We're just down the street from Verge now.

"And how do you two know each other?" Zack asks warily, eyeing me in the mirror.

"Met at your wedding reception, man," I say with a grin. He shakes his head but smiles back.

"And you're working with Myers, and got roped into this case?"

Before he can continue, my phone buzzes, so I take it out of my pocket and glance at it.

Goddamned Nichole again.

Are you getting her or what? You've got important plans that take precedence over your daughter?

I breathe out, trying to keep calm. She knows how to goad me.

You know I'd take Devin every single day if I could. It isn't my weekend, though, so I have to take care of things to make sure I'm home. Sounds to me like I'm not the one whose plans take precedence over his daughter.

Asshole.

I shove my phone back in my pocket just as Zack pulls up in front of Verge.

"Thanks, man. I'm bringing her to the green room. You sure we weren't followed?"

Zack shakes his head. "Nope. Clear."

I take Zoe's bag out of the back, then come around to her side. I don't trust her not to pull something stupid when she's wound up like this, so I take her by the elbow and lead her into the main entryway door. Verge isn't open yet so there is no bouncer at the door, but I'm dungeon monitor tonight. God, I never even made it home yesterday from my night out, and I still have to get to my place to make sure everything's ready for Devin coming tonight.

We move straight past the entryway then past the bar room. Tobias is at the bar, stocking shelves, and he eyes me curiously as I march Zoe past him.

"Tobias. Meet you in your office in ten?" I ask.

"Yeah," he says, crossing his arms on his chest. We keep moving.

"Let go of me," Zoe says. I release her, and she pulls away from me, shooting me a glare. "You can stop manhandling now, you know."

"Not gonna run or try any heroics?" I ask her.

"Of course not." She's frowning, but I ignore her as I take her to the green room.

"So far the only people who know you're here are Zack, Tobias, the owner, and me. You can trust us."

I push open the door, hold it for her to enter, then let it shut with a bang behind us. The room has been cleaned since we left this morning. God, it seems so long ago now.

"I need to get back to my place," I explain. "I have company tonight."

She sits on the edge of the bed and looks around the room, then she looks back at me as if she's just understood what I said.

"Company tonight?" The anger's gone now, and there's a look in her eyes I can't identify.

"Yeah," I say. "My daughter's coming to stay with me."

"Okay. How old is your daughter?"

"Six."

"So it seems I'm not the only one with secrets."

I laugh, as I walk over to the bureau up against the wall, near the bathroom. "Yeah, it's no secret. We've only known each other for hours, though, so there might be a few things about each other we don't know yet."

"Clearly."

I ignore the sarcasm in her tone. "So you can leave your clothes here in the dresser, and I'll make sure you get toiletries in the bathroom. I'll get you food, and whatever else you need."

She nods. "I can't hide in here all the time, you know. I mean, I've got a job to do."

I turn around and face her. I knew this was coming. "Zoe, as we said, you're going to take a leave of absence. Zack will process it. It's too risky for you to go to work until we find who's behind what happened today."

She gets to her feet, shaking her head. "No fucking way. Are you crazy? And who the hell are you to decide this?"

She's right. I don't have a claim on her. I'm not her dom, or even her boyfriend. Still, I'm not gonna let her do stupid shit. Instead of answering her question, I decide to pose some questions of my own. "Do you have a better idea?"

A muscle ticks in her jaw and she looks around the small, but nicely-furnished room. She's silent for a minute before she blows out a breath and sighs. "Well. No," she finally admits. "Not really."

I nod. "Listen, Myers and I are gonna work with Zack

and get to the bottom of this. We'll get them behind bars and you to freedom as soon as we can. But until then, you have to play it safe, Zoe. No heroics or wiseass moves, or stupid-ass shit that'll get you killed. Got it?"

"Fine," she says. "You and Myers and Zack and *me*," she says. "Did you forget I'm in on this, too?"

I shake my head. "No, of course not."

Her gazes sweeps the room, and her eyes pause on the wall filled with implements and tools I use for play time.

"One question, though, *Master* Brax."

I bite back a laugh. She's a spitfire. "Yeah?"

She tilts her head to the side and I'm reminded why I was drawn to her in the first place. Her hair swings and hits her chin, her eyes bright and curious. "When do I get the kink tour?"

Chapter 6

Zoe

God, this place is crazy, like it was lifted out of some scene in a BDSM book or something. The walls are painted a dark hunter green, with a matte finish giving the room a subdued feel. There's a thermostat on the wall set at seventy-two degrees, and though there are three large windows, they're covered in sheer curtains that allow light to filter in yet give the room total privacy. We're on the right side of the club, so all windows face the street. The fridge is stocked with some protein shakes, fruit cups, and bottled water, but little else.

I spent one night here but don't remember much. So now it's time I get myself better acquainted.

Brax went to go tend to things with his daughter, after ordering me lunch and asking me to stay put until he got back. He promised me the deluxe version of a tour when he gets back, and I wonder what that means. Does that include demonstrations? I snicker to myself at my own joke, taking another bite of the pizza. God, I forgot how much I love pizza in NYC. The crust is slightly charred and chewy, the sauce perfectly seasoned with a little tang, the cheese rich and creamy. I eat three slices before I'm full, then slide the remains in the little fridge that's in here. This place is nearly as well furnished as my apartment. Clearly, this is outfitted for extended stays. Among other things.

I make my way to the bathroom and check things out. This is impressive. An enormous, circular tub that must be a whirlpool or something, sits in one corner of the room. It has steps and a sturdy handle leading to it. There's a pile of plush green towels in the closet, as well as an ample stock of hand towels and washcloths. I touch them gingerly with the tip of my finger. They're soft, and they smell faintly of a clean, invigorating mountain-breeze, as if they've been freshly laundered. The bathroom's impeccably clean, but I can't attribute that to Brax, as it's clear someone who does housecleaning was in here before we returned. There's a cabinet next to the towels. Feeling a bit like I'm sneaking into things I shouldn't, I open it. I blink in surprise. There's a full supply of first aid materials here, bandages and ointments, saline, and ibuprofen. Why would he need such a heavy stock of medical supplies? Even as an emergency responder, I have the bare minimum at my apartment. He doesn't even live here.

Are his play sessions… dangerous?

I close it quickly, my heart thumping in my chest.

Why do I sort of hope they are? Why does the thought of him doing dangerous things make my pulse race?

I leave the bathroom and shut off the light, returning to the main area. I was so plastered when I came here last, I don't really remember much except for a really, *really* large bed, some things hanging on the wall, and the dark green color of the walls. It was nighttime and darker, so I didn't really see everything he has in here. And hell, does he have this place outfitted.

I walk to where the array of things hangs from pegs on the wall. I may not be a kink expert, but even I know these are things designed to cause pain. How much pain? I have no idea. But the varnished wooden paddle-like thing with holes drilled into it doesn't look like it'll tickle. It appears he has them arranged according to type. Beside the paddle hangs a thinner wooden thing that looks way more flexible, like some type of rod. Gingerly, I take it down, and tap it against my palm. I inhale sharply, surprised at how much such a flimsy little thing like this hurts. For some reason, I tap my palm a second time, a line of fire lighting across my skin. I'm not sure why I need to do this. I didn't think I like pain. But the thought of Brax wielding this on me makes my mouth go dry. I hang it back up and flex my palm, trying to ease the pain.

There are several other things that look like hairbrushes without bristles, stouter paddles, and something that resembles a back scratcher, but it's far longer and more wicked-looking. Next to the wooden things hang a bunch of items that are leather-wrapped. I draw closer, inhaling the fragrance while I gently touch the first. It looks similar to the paddle, but it's covered in deep crimson leather, with beautiful intricate roses carved into the leather. Beside that hangs what looks like a strap, black and sturdy, with little give to it, like a belt of sorts. Some of the leather things are soft and some sturdier. I lift the rose-covered paddle and smack my palm with it. It has a very different sort of feel than the thin, flexible thing. It stings, but it's almost pleasant, leaving behind a warm burn. I look around me, suddenly tempted to try this thing out. No one will see me. I have no doubt I'm in total privacy here, or he never would have brought me here to begin with. I want to feel this thing. I reach behind me and whack my own ass with the rose thing, feeling like a total moron.

My cheeks flame with embarrassment. I can't believe I just spanked my own ass. But I like the way the paddle feels and make a mental note to somehow talk Brax into giving that one a go on me.

I go down the line and look at the rest of the things on the wall. There are some plastic ones that look wicked, a black loopy thing that makes me cringe, and a small table to the far right houses a variety of things that make me stare. I can identify rubber-tipped clamp-things attached to a chain, leather cuffs, and a variety of things that look like they're meant to tie someone up—a length of soft, braided rope, a silky blindfold with a thin elastic attached like something one might wear to bed at night to block out light, and even a pair of lightweight plastic zip ties. I look at them in bewilderment. Really? Then I remember what Brax said about bondage being his specialty.

But there's something besides the ropes and ties that catches my attention, and not in a good way. It looks almost like a hood, but with an area cut out for breathing. My heart thunders in my chest and it isn't until I notice I'm lightheaded and grasping the table that I take a huge, deep breath. I was holding my breath. The feeling of suffocating has my anxiety mounting. I close my eyes and will myself to calm.

I can't bear anything that deprives me of the ability to breathe deeply. Being punished by being locked in a closet will do that to someone. I hate that I'm weak like that, and I've done everything I can to get myself over it, but I can't. Just the thought of that damn hood over my head for whatever the fuck reason makes me feel like someone's squeezing the breath out of my lungs. I take several more deep breaths before I drop the lid to the table, and move on.

There are two padded pieces of furniture in here. How did I not notice them before? Or did he have them put in here? Either option is admittedly disconcerting. He didn't have time to have them put in here, so I suppose they were cast in darkness, as they're in the furthest corner of the room and from a distance they make it look like a place to sit and read or something. But that's clearly not what these are. One is a padded bench that looks like some kind of modified kneeler someone might find at church, but something tells me this is not used for praying. And to the right of that lies a flat table that's slightly bent, almost like a recliner. Next to that table sits an assortment of candles. I look at them curiously. They seem really out of place here. Why does he have enough candles in here he could open up a shop? Brax doesn't seem like the hippie sort. I shake my head. The questions just keep piling up.

I walk back to the bed and feel exhaustion weighing me down. It's comfortable and quiet in here, and I didn't get much sleep the night before. The pizza filled my belly, and now I feel like I could take a nap. After I dress into a pair of yoga pants and a cami, I lay down on the huge bed. It isn't until I'm half-asleep, looking at the room around me, when I notice rings attached to the posts of the bed. I swallow hard, the vision of me attached to those rings making me feel warm and tingly inside. What would he do to me if I were fastened to those rings? Would I like it?

My body says *hell yeah I would*.

I wish I had my computer. My phone will do, but it's not as easy to do searches as it is on my laptop. And hell, do I have shit to look up. I know almost nothing about kink clubs except that there are things like *tops* and *bottoms*, doms and subs and… other things. He's not only spanked me, he's threatened to, and he's already made it clear he's a self-professed dom. So what exactly *is* a dom?

I take out my phone and begin to Google, but my eyelids are heavy and I can't keep my eyes open. I fall into a dreamless sleep.

"WAKE *UP,* SLEEPING BEAUTY."

I mumble and moan, twisting up in the sheets and pulling the pillow over my head. I hate waking up.

"Deja vu here." Brax's deep voice, laced with laughter, gets my attention. Wait. Where am I? I pull the pillow off my head and blink up at him. It's dark outside the windows.

"How long did I sleep?" I ask, pushing myself up to sitting, and rubbing the sleep from my eyes.

He sits on the edge of the bed. "I don't know," he says with a chuckle. "I'm sorry I was later than I expected. Had to wait for a sitter for Devin, but she's all set now. I came back as soon as I could. It's not supposed to be my weekend with her, but I had to pinch hit."

I nod. "So your daughter's taken care of," I say, my voice still straggly from sleep. "And she's six. And you have, lemme guess, a crazy ex."

He rolls his eyes. "Yep."

Great. I landed myself a man with a crazy ex.

Wait. He's not my man.

I nod. "Okay, then. So when are you going to give me the tour?" I ask.

He looks away and his jaw firms. "Not sure that's the best idea now," he says. "Has Zack been in here to talk to you?"

"No." I'm immediately on alert. I sit up, frowning at him. "What the hell is going on?"

He looks at me steadily, his voice grim. "While I was gone there was a disturbance at your building. Not sure what happened, but all I know is NYPD officers showed up, there was an altercation, and your doorman ended up shot."

Jesus. Reynolds? The doorman?

"Wait. What?"

"So far news says the doorman was involved in some kinda illicit activity, NYPD tried to apprehend him, he put up a fight and pulled a weapon."

"Reynolds wouldn't hurt a flea," I whisper, shaking my head. "This is bullshit. He kept dog treats behind the desk to hand to the little spoiled terrier on the fourth floor. He planted flowers on Memorial Day for the wounded vets and volunteered at the Big Brothers and Sisters Association. Is he okay?"

Brax looks away. "No."

Christ.

I pinch the bridge of my nose. "Where's Zack?"

"Zack's looking into it, and he'll see you tonight." He clears his throat. "He's bringing Beatrice with him. I want you to talk to her about doing something with your hair. Something radically different. Dying it, maybe. Cutting it." He gently runs his fingers through the tangled hair on the pillow.

"What?"

"Listen, Zoe. We have no idea who knows *what* here. None. Zack is confident no one tracked you here to Verge, but we have to keep your staying here an absolute secret. You do not venture outside of this club until we figure out what the hell is going on and just how deeply this corruption goes. You get me?"

Yeah, right. If he thinks I'm going to hide like some sorta scared little girl, he's got another think coming. I'll play along, though.

"You want me to dye my hair," I repeat, nodding my head. "Fine. If you think that's what I should do."

"I do. I'm going to meet with Myers in thirty minutes, debrief him on everything we know, and have his men look into this. You can trust him. He and his men will find out what we need to know."

"You mean what *you* need to know. I do jack shit sitting in here like some kind of criminal." It sounds petulant and I know it, but I'm pissed. I hate that I have to go in hiding to protect my ass when the real criminals wander free.

Brax reaches over to me and brushes my hair off my forehead. "You're beautiful when you're angry. You know that?"

I don't respond. I'm not sure what to say. Looking around his room and lying in his bed, I want to remember what happened last night. I want to feel his hands on me again. I might not remember every detail, but I do remember that it was *really* fucking good.

"Thanks," I say with a sigh. "I hate this, Brax. I don't want to hide, and I feel totally useless in here."

He shakes his head. "You're not useless. You've given us enough information to go on for now. We have names. Your biggest goal is staying *alive*, Zoe. What makes you think you're any different from Zandetti? From Reynolds?"

"Fine," I finally agree. I cross my arms on my chest and look around the room. "You've got a lot of explaining to do when you get back," I mutter. "I wanna know what all this is."

He chuckles and playfully slaps the side of my leg. "Will do. Now sit tight and wait for Beatrice. Do *not* leave this room under any condition. You get me?"

"Yeah," I say, though I have every intention of leaving this room and investigating things for myself, namely, exactly what kind of whiskey Verge stocks behind that bar. I won't be a dumbass about it, though. Still, I'm no wallflower and I won't pretend to be.

He looks thoughtfully at me, then leans down and to my surprise, presses a kiss to my forehead. It's so sweet it makes tears prick my eyes. I look away so he doesn't see.

"I'll be back as soon as I can. I've got a shift here tonight, but I'll check in on you. Keep your phone on you. Myers will want information. If the club was closed, I'd take you with me but leaving now might rouse suspicion and we don't want that." He gets to his feet and his voice drops to the deep, commanding register he uses when he means business. "Stay here, Zoe. You understand?"

"Sure."

"Anything you need? Some more to eat?"

"No, I'm good. Could use a drink."

A corner of his lips quirks up, but his eyes look a little troubled. "We'll talk about that when I get back."

What the hell does that mean?

He leaves, and I wait a little while before I get out of bed. I close my eyes briefly.

Reynolds.

They got Reynolds. How far does this go? How deep is the corruption? I feel like Ben Hoffman's only the very tip of the iceberg.

I need a disguise. But I also need a drink before Zack and Beatrice arrive. I'll think clearer when I've had a little drink and am able to push away the pain that claws at my chest when memories surface. I became who I am to seek justice, and hell, I'm not gonna find justice sitting here on my ass.

I sift through my bag until I find an oversized top I

usually wear to bed that will cover my curves and make me look bigger than I am, and a pair of worn, nondescript jeans. There's a baseball cap hanging on the wall in the back of the room, and I have enough make-up in my bag I can disguise myself well. Even Zack or Beatrice won't recognize me.

When I'm done, I give myself a once-over in the mirror in the bathroom. No one would ever think this is me.

Tentatively, I open the door, but then I realize that if I'm creeping around and being hesitant about anything, that I might look suspicious. I finish opening the door with confidence, and when I let it go, it shuts firmly behind me. I turn, panic-stricken, and realize with chagrin that it fucking locked behind me. What the hell is that about? Jesus. How am I going to get back in there and pretend I never left? Something tells me I don't want to face Brax when he's angry.

Ah well. I'll worry about that later. I walk with confidence in the direction of the bar. I have a good head for directions and remember the layout of the club. The private rooms are apart from a room that has like ten times as much equipment as Brax's private play area, but beyond the rooms lies the bar.

The main area is crowded with people in various states of dress when I arrive. Some wear nothing but leather, some scantily clad with only strips of material covering their crotches or breasts. I'm supposed to fit in here, so I don't gape, but I wish I could really spend some time looking around. I realize pretty quickly that my stupid outfit meant to look casual and unremarkable isn't a disguise at all. I stick out in this crowd dressed like this. *Shit.*

I look to the bar. My mouth waters. Jesus, I need a shot.

I make my way there trembling, not from fear but the sudden need that consumes me as I draw closer. I need to taste the fiery burn. I need to feel it burn my throat and into my belly, giving me the relief I need.

"Hey," I say, casting my eyes down when I reach the bar. I'd look out of place here if people weren't so uniquely dressed. I might not be dressed in leathers, but it doesn't really look like there's a dress code here, and no one really looks my way.

"Get you a drink?" The bartender asks before he swipes the counter with a bar mop.

"Redbreast neat, please," I say. I can't give him Zack or Braxton's name, because that might make him suspicious.

"Your name?"

"Mary." *Lame. God.*

"Nice to meet you, Mary," the bartender says, extending a hand. "Name's Travis."

He hands me my drink and I thank him. The key to staying anonymous is making sure that I don't linger anywhere too long so I need to move. I can tell from what I've seen that money doesn't exchange hands here. I guess it's hard to carry cash when you're not wearing much of anything for clothes. I have to make sure no one knows I'm here, though. Then I remember the locked door.

"I'm a guest of Master Tobias," I say, not making eye contact with the bartender. "He said to put my drink on his tab."

I won't make eye contact with the bartender, but his voice makes me want to leave, and now. He's clearly suspicious.

"Guest of Tobias?" he repeats, and in front of me he anchors his hands on his hips.

"Yes. Thanks so much," I say, making my way away from the bar and toward the other area of this room and far, far away from the bartender. I wonder if he's a dominant, too. Seems those guys aren't so good at believing fibs. And Brax said he had a shift here tonight. What does he do again? Is he one of those guys dressed in leather? The very idea makes me giggle to myself nervously.

Where the hell am I?

From here, this place looks like a normal club, with pool tables and a dance floor. Then I see a couple approach. He's wearing a chain and collar, and she's dressed in all black, wearing a pair of stilettos. I can't imagine walking in shoes like that, much less leading some guy on a chain behind me, but she does it with grace as she approaches the bar.

"Pinot Grigio for me," she orders. "And a bowl of water for Slave."

I blink.

What the fuck?

I will not judge I will not judge I will not judge, I chant to myself, turning away from them. Hey, whatever floats their boats or whatever the fuck. I drain the rest of my drink and realize I need to find a quiet, secluded area. I can't get back into the room, but I really don't need to be on display, either.

"My guest?" I hear a stern, deep voice speaking from the bar area. *Shit.* As cautiously as I can, I crane my neck to see Brax's friend, the one he called Tobias, speaking to Travis at the bar. Tobias is frowning. He's gonna give me away and then it'll cause a scene and how the hell am I going to handle this now? Why the fuck did I do this, anyway? The ice clinks in the glass in my hand, and I remember why.

Why the fuck do I need this? I hate that I do. I don't like being dependent on anyone or any*thing.* Tomorrow, I won't touch the stuff. I can handle my shit without the aid of something to numb my senses.

Tobias frowns, looking around the bar, then he sees me. I look away quickly, but it's too late. Brax has told him I'm here and I saw recognition in that sober gaze of his.

He starts to come my way, in long strides, and I don't have any answers for him. If I have to talk to him then Brax will know I left the room, and the last thing I need is to make it obvious I'm here. I swear under my breath, turn away from Tobias, then turn into the crush of people by the pool tables. I walk quicker and only after I've stepped far away, look over my shoulder. Tobias hasn't lost sight of me, though. What will he do if he catches me?

I quickly skirt between the couples and head for the hallway that will take me to a much busier room. I can see from where I stand there will be serious kink at play there, and I can't imagine Tobias will want to cause a scene. I don't see him following me now, and it feels like I'm totally free. Quickly, I race into the room then nearly halt in my tracks.

If I thought I was underdressed in the main area? It's abundantly clear in the dungeon.

Ho-ly *SHIT*.

This place is... unreal. There are padded tables and others that are shaped oddly, like horses, as well as v-shaped tables and a variety of furniture that looks like a variation of an examination table someone might find in a doctor's office. Along one wall hangs an assortment of wooden beams that form crosses, rings hanging from the ends, and couples are in various states of kink play.

I flinch at the sound of something solid hitting flesh, and I turn around, almost scared to see what's causing the noise when the strike is following by a wail. Someone has been cuffed to one of the benches, and she looks weirdly young. She's got pig-tails and a frilly, lace-edged skirt, with Mary Janes on her feet. The man behind her looks scary as hell with a shaved head and tattoos snaking around his neck. He's easily a foot taller than she is, his inked arms enormous and muscular, and in his hand, he's got a solid wooden paddle. He bends down and whispers something in her ear. She nods and grins, then he's behind her with his hand on her lower back. I can't watch. It seems too private for me to be here watching, like being in the room with someone having sex.

Then why does my pussy contract when the man wraps his hand in her head and pulls her head back? Why does my clit pulse with arousal when the sturdy paddle connects with the girl's ass?

Far to the right, in a darker corner of the room, I see someone… dangling? Confused, I walk as casually as I can closer to get a better look, which is maybe not so smart since now I'm further away from the exit, and I need a quick escape route. But I want to see what the hell is going on in here.

There's a man below, holding something small and flexible in his hand, and the woman beside him is literally strung up in some sort of rope. I can see where the woven strands cross her bare breasts, and even though I have never seen anything like this in my life, I'm fascinated. It isn't that the woman is nearly naked, wearing only the tiniest thong, but the look on her face. She looks at total peace. I swallow hard.

What would it be like to give up control like this? To have it physically restricted from me? Behind me I hear the sound of flesh being struck again, and though I jump at the sound, an electric thrill runs down my spine. I notice one man and a woman walking around as if they're in charge, detached from all play and without a partner. Are they what Brax referred to as dungeon monitors? I try to observe them without being seen myself, when something gets my attention. A woman is sprawled on the table that looks like it belongs in an exam room, her legs tied down spread-eagle, but that doesn't bother me. It's what's on her head that does. It's black, like a mask, with a small circular opening for her mouth. Panic strikes me just seeing her wear it. How can she handle that over her face like that? I imagine she's cast into total darkness and can't hear anything. I suppose that's the point of that hood.

I clutch at my chest and anger rises in me. I'm not a weakling who loses her shit over things like this. I've been in seriously dangerous situations that don't make my heart trip in my chest like this. And why does my body have to respond like this?

A part of me goes into automatic cop mode but I have to suppress it. The people here *want* this. Hell, it's even legal. I'm the one that has issues.

"Excuse me." The deep voice in my ear nearly makes me scream, but at least I draw in breath. I turn to see Tobias glaring down at me. "Not sure we've had the pleasure of meeting." Damn, this was not how I wanted to meet the guy.

I extend my hand but don't give him my name. I can't speak freely here but I need him on my side. I lean in close and whisper, "I'm with Braxton. He had to run out but he's coming back, and I just stepped out of the room for a minute."

Tobias shakes my hand quickly, eyeing me with a gaze that pierces right through me. He releases my hand and crosses his arms on his chest. He's intimidating, tall and serious-looking.

"I'm friends with Zack, too, and he can vouch for me," I whisper. "Please. Don't cause a scene."

He raises a brow, but a corner of his lips twitches upward. He leans in and whispers, "I'll leave the scening to Master Braxton. Just took me a minute to realize who it was that put her drink on my tab."

"I'll pay you back," I hiss. "I'm not trying to take advantage of you, I swear. I just didn't have any cash and it didn't look like anyone was handing any over. I was afraid if I mentioned Brax people would get suspicious."

"I don't care about the tab," he says. "I care that you're out here, when Brax promised me you wouldn't be."

I sigh. "Look, I didn't mean to come in here," I say, but my protest sounds silly and weak. "I only wanted to step out for a minute, but I didn't realize the door would lock behind me."

He's still frowning and doesn't reply. I continue on stupidly. "So I decided to look around a little while I wait for him to return. But since you're here, maybe you can let me back in the green room?" I give him my most winning smile, but he's still not amused, staring at me with one brow raised now.

"It's safest for you if you're back in that room," he says in a voice so low no one but me can hear him. "But I think I'll let Master Braxton handle you." He jerks his chin at the same time I feel a strong hand grip my upper arm.

"I think that's an excellent idea," Brax's voice murmurs in my ear. He continues in a voice so low it's almost a purr. "You walk with me and don't cause a scene. I want you as inconspicuous as possible. You've already seriously crossed a line." He looks up at Tobias. "She do anything I need to be aware of?" I hate the way they're talking about me as if I'm not even here, but I don't want to cause a scene, so I bite my lip, even though I'm fuming.

Tobias shrugs. "We'll talk about it later."

What the fuck?

Brax is marching me out of here now. "I told you stay put," he says in a low growl. The way he's talking to me and the grip he has on my arm, makes me feel like a naughty child and I don't like it. I hate the weight that presses on my chest with the knowledge I've screwed up and someone's mad at me.

"Whatever," I mutter, angry at him. I'm trying with everything I've got to hold my shit together, so I have to turn into bitch mode or I'm gonna lose my mind and I *can't* lose my mind. I'll cry. Jesus, I hate when I cry. I was an idiot for coming out here to begin with.

He takes out the keys to the green room and glances casually around us. It's just us here now, though, the sounds of the dungeon fading as he pushes the door open to the private room and ushers me inside. The door shuts with an audible click behind him.

"What the *fuck*, Zoe," he growls, prowling in the room and releasing my arm. I rub the place where he grasped me, not because it hurts so much as I need to make myself feel better about this. I hate how I feel. I hate how I'm a little girl shamed. This isn't me anymore. Fuck it, *this isn't me.*

There's this maddening weight between us because I've fucked up and he's angry with me. I can't look at him, because then I'm afraid somehow he'll *see* that little girl inside who's ashamed. As much as I try to cover her up with my fierce confidence and strength, she's there, and if he looks me in the eyes, he'll see her.

"I just wanted a drink, Braxton, for fuck's sake," I mutter, but he doesn't say anything at first. I risk a look at him. It surprises me when I look at him that the anger has already faded, and in its place is a milder look. His eyes no longer flash but look sad, but not quite. It's worse than anger. He looks disappointed. His lips turn down, his arms still crossed on his chest.

To my surprise, he crooks a finger at me. "Come here," he says.

To my further surprise, my heart stutters in my chest and my mouth is as dry as the Sahara. I blink at him, but he still doesn't get angry, just repeats in the same low, determined voice, "Come here, Zoe."

I walk over to him, a weight on my chest like a treasure chest, heavy and solid, my mind a jumble of hurt and anger and confusion. What the hell are we doing here? He's a guy who means nothing to me. A one-night stand is just that: one night of passion and sex and heat, no strings attached. And yet here I am, in his private room, locked away from danger, and as I draw close to him, I focus on the fact that he's a dominant.

What exactly does that mean? He has all sorts of toys and things stashed around this room, but what does that *mean?* What does a dominant do? And if he's a dom, what does that make me?

I somehow reach him and when I do, he uncrosses his arms and takes my chin between his fingers. My lips tremble, and the weight on my chest loosens a little. The touch of his fingers on my chin reminds me of the imbalance of power here. By crossing the room to him, I've granted him something, though I'm not yet sure what.

"It was dumb," I whisper, and to my utter horror, my eyes dampen. *Fuck.* I'm not the girl who cries. What is it about this guy that breaks down my walls? "And dangerous." I'm a trained officer. I've been taught, and seen firsthand, that bravery doesn't come on the tail of stupidity. We're trained to wait for back-up, go in properly armed, and only the dumbasses wander into dangerous situations without proper weapons or back-up.

I fucked up today. Big time.

But I think what really makes me feel badly is the knowledge that this guy has put himself on the line for me. He's here to protect me, and doing everything he can, and I couldn't follow the simplest of directives. And that makes me feel like an idiot.

"God, I'm stupid," I blurt out, attempting to shake my head so I can look away from him, but he holds my chin fast.

"You're not stupid," Brax says firmly. "I don't ever want to hear you say that again."

I swallow and try to nod but can't because of the whole chin grip thing.

"You're strong and brave and willful as fuck," he says, icy blue eyes blazing with fire and conviction. Something loosens in my chest even further, and I begin to tremble, but before I can form a thought, his mouth crashes on mine, a punishing kiss that brands me with its vehemence, a clash of tongues and breath that would make my knees give out if he didn't grab the small of my back and hold me against him. Too soon, he pulls away, his mouth to my ear. "You need to be punished," he whispers, making me whimper with heat and arousal.

He sits heavily on the bed and brings me between his knees, his eyes on mine as his fingers unfasten my jeans. The heat of the moment makes blood pound in my ears and down my chest, skittering down my belly and right between my thighs. I'm aflame and trembling, incapable of anything but following his lead. One of his hands snakes around the back of my neck, pulling me in for another kiss, while his other hand pushes down my jeans. I feel them pool around my feet, and he stops kissing me long enough to whisper, "Step out of them and lay over my lap."

It's as if he possesses me. I don't really have control

over this situation. I'm aroused and nervous and admittedly mildly curious. Why does the knowledge he's about to discipline me make me feel so many strange, unfamiliar things? I can't even begin to decipher them, as he's drawing me over his knee. My heart thunders in my chest, my arousal coating my thighs, but a part of me can't breathe for nerves.

He presses me over his lap, my belly resting against the warmth of his thighs, and before I'm even settled, his hand crashes down in a stinging *slap* that makes the breath whoosh right out of me. A second smack follows the first, followed by a crisp spank on my upper thighs. I writhe with both pain and need, a low throb between my thighs pulsing along with the heat on my ass.

"You may be a strong, capable officer out *there*," he says, punctuating his words with sharp smacks of his palm. "But in here, you're mine."

Am I?

"So that means you get to spank me?" I protest, wiggling because fuck it hurts, even if in a dim part of my brain I still want him to do it.

"Hell yes it does," he says with a growl, giving me one rapid spank after another. I writhe but he holds me fast until he's given me a dozen hard spanks with his hand. God, it throbs and burns like a million bee stings. I can't even imagine what those other things feel like if this is just his palm.

And then he's done. I'm panting, exhausted, over his lap, my eyes closed on the bed while he massages my flaming hot skin. I hiss when he kneads my abused flesh, but at the very same time I can feel how badly I need him. My nipples are hard, my pussy throbbing, and I want the hand that's on my ass to touch me lower.

He doesn't touch me, though. Not yet. He turns me

over his lap and cradles me up on his chest, my scorched, bare ass on his thighs, and even though I'm horny as hell, I need this. I bury my face in his chest and realize right then, as his large, strong arms encircle me, that this very well may be the first time anyone's ever held me. I was never touched with gentleness like this in foster care, but slapped and belittled, and that was oh so different from what he just did. My boyfriends kissed me and fucked me, and I'm no virgin, but no one was ever… a *cuddler*. I'm not even sure I am. But here, on his lap, after being stripped emotionally, and being held like this, I feel so many things I don't even begin to know how to figure it all out.

"That was so embarrassing," I say, without even meaning to. "God, I feel so… I don't even know."

"That's okay. You don't need to know," he says, holding me tight. He's even rocking a little, as if he needs this as much as I do, this comfort and intimacy. "And really, I'm not too worried about you being embarrassed." His gritty voice rumbles over me. "Maybe that'll make you think twice before you act. Listen, Zoe. I'm not gonna hold you in here forever." He bends his head down. The too-big top I'm wearing has slipped to the side, baring my shoulder. He plants a warm, firm kiss on the tattoo there. "Jesus, baby, you've got wings. You need to fly. And I won't be the one to hold you back. But we just need to figure things out."

I nod.

"I need to keep you safe," he whispers. "I had a good talk with Myers, and he's looking into things. Tomorrow we'll check out the leads we've got." He nips the tattoo, igniting the flames he stoked when he spanked me.

I nod. Yeah, yeah, whatever. Bad guys and shit and investigation. I just need him to keep doing what he's doing.

He suckles my skin in his mouth, then lies me on the bed on my back. Blue eyes boring into mine, he tugs the crumpled jeans that hang around my ankles and tosses them to the floor. I feel like I'm wearing a nightgown or something, dressed only in this enormous top.

He leans over and drags his tongue along my skin. "You taste delicious," he growls. "Fucking delectable."

"Delectable," I repeat with a giggle as his tongue continues to caress my neck.

"Mhm," he murmurs, leaning over me and pressing his warm, heavy body against mine. "Those nipples peaked for me, sweetheart?"

"Oh I don't know, there was this really hot guy in that room with all the tables—ow!"

I don't expect the slap that lands on my thigh. "Dude, that hurt."

"I'll give you hurt."

"You already did!"

He shakes his head. "Maybe that was a warm-up," he says, working his mouth down my neck to my collar bone, trailing the tip of his tongue in warm, sensual swipes. "Maybe you need more. I have some toys in that box over there…"

"Oh my God I know."

His raspy chuckle makes my nipples pebble. "Got a chance to explore, did you?" he asks.

"You could say that—aaaaahhhh." I lose the ability to speak as now he's lifted my top, the fabric bunching, and his tongue is now swirling deliciously along my navel while his calloused thumbs graze my nipples.

"You need more, baby?" he asks. "Go ahead. Beg."

"You son of a bitch," I say with a laugh. "Anyone ever tell you you're a control freak?" I playfully slap at him, but he grabs my hands and entwines his fingers in mine, pinning my hands to the bed. "Baby, you're incorrigible," he says. "Knew I should've spanked you harder. Should've used my belt."

"Mmmm," I moan.

"Should've whipped your ass," he says with a chuckle, biting the sensitive skin at my side, a sting of pain that only ignites my fire.

"Dude, laughing while you threaten to whip my ass isn't gonna really get the point across."

He pushes himself up and his brows furrow, his lips turn down in a frown and suddenly my dimpled-tormentor looks stern as fuck. "That better?"

I blink and don't respond, so he gives me a wicked grin. "That's what I thought." Eyes on me, he lowers his mouth to my nipple while his hand dips between my thighs.

Oh. Fuck. Yes. My eyes roll back in my head and I throw my head back.

"That's it," he coaxes as my back arches. "Take it, babygirl. Chase it. You took your punishment so now you take what's yours. Milk those fingers and let yourself fly."

It's all I need. At the first stroke of his fingers I was ready to come, and now I can hardly keep myself from losing total control.

His raspy, sexy voice pushes me over the edge and I come with abandon, tossing my head back as I scream his name and he milks every last drop of bliss from me. I fall back on the bed, suddenly exhausted. I can hardly move. I can barely even *think*.

He lies down beside me and pulls me up next to him. I breathe him in and just lie here.

"All better?" he asks.

"That your gig? You punish girls and then make them climax and call it a day?" I'm teasing him, but there's a hint of jealousy in my voice even I recognize. I don't like the idea of him with another girl.

He only growls in response and changes the subject.

"You look around this room?" he asks, a smile tipping his lips up and that adorable dimple showing.

"Oh yeah," I say, scrambling back on the bed to get more comfortable. "Checked out alllll the kinky toys."

He chuckles, a low, sexy sound that makes me smile myself. The way he hitches his thumbs in the loops on his jeans makes my stomach do a little flip, like he's only playing casual but capable of much, much more. My mind immediately goes to the spanking he gave me in my kitchen, the tug of his fingers in my hair, the night we spent together.

One corner of his lips quirks up. "And anything interest you?"

I shrug. "Maybe? I don't know." I need to throw up my walls. My voice tightens as I speak to him. "I'll tell you one thing that *doesn't*. Keep that hood away from me. No hoods. I don't know what the fuck they're for, but I want no part of that."

He sobers, the smile leaving his eyes and his shoulders noticeably tense. "Hood?"

I swallow. "Well, there's some kinda black thing in there."

He pushes off the bed and walks over to the other side of the room, then opens the case where I was investigating earlier. "Oh yeah. I forgot about that. I never used it. Don't need to. I'd prefer just telling you to close your eyes and making sure you did what you were told."

"I saw a crazy looking hood in the kinky room," I say, earning a growl from him. Oh yeah. I wasn't supposed to be in that room. Oops.

"Want to tell me what else you saw in the dungeon?" he asks sternly.

Hearing him say "dungeon" makes my reality sink in.

I'm so in over my head.

"I saw a lot of things," I say truthfully. "And really, Brax, I have no idea what the hell most of it is."

"Good," he says, looking strangely pleased. "So did you see a black hood with a hole cut into it in the dungeon?"

I heart pounds just listening to him talk about it. "Yeah. What the hell is that?"

"Sensory deprivation hood," he says. "It's… maybe a little more hardcore than you're used to. Not sure. Takes away sight and sound and scent… well, everything but the ability to breathe, really."

"Looks fucking terrifying."

"Some bottoms really like them."

"Ok, so I don't think you're talking about my ass." I've looked some things up, but I want to hear his explanation.

He sits on the edge of the bed. "A top is the one in control in a scene, and a bottom is the one on the receiving end."

"Oh. So I'm the bottom? That's weird."

He snorts. "If it helps, you're a very cute bottom."

I smile and close my eyes. It's been a long fucking day and I need some rest. Tomorrow, I find out what Myers knows and check in with Zack. For now, I just need some sleep.

I feel the bed rise as he gets to his feet. "I have to go to the dungeon. I'm on tonight, but I'm going home early."

I nod. "Okay." I'm curious what he does as dungeon monitor, and part of me wonders if there's any way I can sneak in and see, when his voice cuts into my thoughts.

"And don't you even *think* about coming in there. You

got it?" His harsh tone catches my attention and I open my eyes back up.

"Who, me?"

"Zoe," he says, hands anchored on his hips as he glares at me. "I catch you leaving this room and you'll wish you hadn't. I've taken it easy on you. *Way* too easy on you. Got it?"

"Got it."

I'm not his submissive and I won't obey him. But tonight, I can play along.

Chapter 7

Brax

I'm a douchebag for taking advantage of her. I know this.

I decide it won't happen again.

Two days pass, then three, and Myers has done shit all to help shed light on what's going on. He says he's investigated every possible angle, and despite the promise to help clarify what our problem is, he's spinning his wheels. I visit Zoe every chance I can get. She's getting stir crazy, though, I know. I brought her some books and gave her access to a spare laptop Tobias had in his office, but she looks angrier and angrier every time I go to see her.

Zack's been held up on a case, but finally, I get ahold of him. We've had to put off her transformation, which means she's had to stay in the room more or less, and she's not happy about it. Today, Beatrice will do magic with her hair, and then she should get a little of her freedom back. We sit at the bar area, and her eyes keep roaming over there, as if she feels the pull of the alcohol. I suspect she hasn't been keeping away.

"Zack, please, tell me what the fuck is going on," Zoe says, leaning back in the little chair on the side of the circular red table. Zack frowns at her tone. He doesn't like when Beatrice swears, but he won't say anything to Zoe. At least, he'd better not. She's mine, and she's allowed to say whatever the fuck she wants to.

I blink, surprised at the possessive flair that wells in my chest unbidden.

Zack runs a hand through his sandy hair and blows out a breath. "For starters, your job is secure. As far as the NYPD knows, you're on a leave of absence for a family emergency with an indefinite return date. So far everyone's bought that without question, and there's no need for us to push that further."

Her lips thin. "Fair enough." Her face looks a little paler, and there are dark circles under her eyes. Is she sleeping badly? I wouldn't know. I've kept contact with her to a bare minimum, so I can keep her safe and keep my fucking hands off her at the same time. "At least I don't have to worry about that."

"I think at this point it's best for us to investigate on our own. We don't know who we can trust within the NYPD and contacting anyone there puts you at serious risk."

"Of course." Zoe agrees.

"Can you tell me what you know, and maybe we can start putting things together? Let's take it from where we left off," Zack says. "Pretend I know nothing and start from the top."

"Yeah, of course," she says. "So I was dating Ben Hoffman a few months ago when I was in grad school, taking one of Zandetti's courses. One night I was at his house, and I intercepted a text that instructed him to end the life of Zandetti. Next day, the professor went missing and was later found dead. I know he had a wife, but I don't know anything about her. I do know these people were targets, and that's why they were killed."

I nod. This much I can fill in.

"Right. I know a little more about her," I say.

For some reason Zoe's jaw tightens and her eyes go impossibly narrower. What the hell?

"Go on," she says in a voice laden with sarcasm. "Do tell."

Zack seems to ignore her anger, as his gaze is fixed firmly on me. I want to know what the fuck she's so pissed about though. I ignore her glare—we'll get to the bottom of *that* later—and instead I explain to Zack what I've found out.

"First, Daniel Zandetti, our victim. He was named academic specialist at NYCU and he was given millions in grant money. Seventy-five percent of that came from Homeland Security. He was on a whole bunch of major panels. Zandetti knew there was a breach in security and illegal drugs were crossing the border. This is all on public record."

Zack pipes in. "Antonia Zandetti, a journalism professor, worked closely with an investigative reporter she was tight with. After Zandetti's death, both the reporter and Antonia Zandetti went missing."

Zoe nods. "And no one's heard from either one of them since."

I don't realize I'm clenching my fists until I see my hand, white-knuckled and fisted under the table.

Two now dead. Two gone missing, likely also victim to whoever breached security or whoever Zandetti targeted. And one woman caught in the crossfire, who sits at the table now in front of me and only because I'm making her. If she had her way she'd be on the street this very minute, guns blazing, ready to take down the ones responsible for the deaths of innocents.

"Not exactly," a voice startles us all, as Beatrice comes into the bar area from the private rooms, where she was preparing a makeshift hair salon. Her blonde hair is tucked into a bun at the nape of her neck, giving us a clear view of her slightly-flushed cheeks. "Did you say Antonia Zandetti?"

"Beatrice," Zack warns. He keeps his wife out of all of his detective work, both for legal and safety reasons.

Beatrice looks at him. Damn, I know that look. She's as feisty as Zoe for Christ's sake. "Zack, I wasn't eavesdropping and up until like thirty seconds ago I had no idea what was going on. But I heard you mention Antonia Zandetti."

Zack grunts, and we all wait for her to continue. Zoe looks especially curious.

"I knew her. She was a client of mine." Beatrice looks to Zoe. "Associate professor at NYCU, right? Tiny woman with thick black hair, olive skin, and a really fit little figure? She was a runner."

Zoe nods. "Yup. That was her."

"She *did* go missing at the time of her husband's death, but her body was never found. I know because the girls at the salon and I read everything we could get our hands on regarding her disappearance. But there was something we knew that never made it to the papers."

Zack raises a curious brow and Zoe leans in closer as Beatrice continues, her eyes bright. "Antonia was having an affair with a man who owned property on Cape Cod. I know this might sound far-fetched, but you need to realize that people treat their hairdressers like they're part-confidante and part-shrink. We know whose kid got into what college, who's filing bankruptcy, and who's having an affair. People are loose lipped while in our chairs."

Zoe nods. "This is true. So you think it's possible Antonia sought safety with the man she was sleeping with? And she isn't dead?"

Beatrice shrugs. "I have no idea. But it's an avenue you might want to pursue." She looks steadily at Zack. "Do you have any other leads?"

Zack's eyes narrow on her. "That's not for you to know, Beatrice." He stands up. "Why don't you two go take care of Zoe's hair and Brax and I will look into this."

Beatrice nods, but Zoe's on her feet, glaring at Zack. "We women can go take care of *hair* and you *menfolk* will go take care of the real business? Is that what you're saying? For fuck's sake, Zack, is this 1952?"

Now it's my turn to wade in. "Zoe, leave it," I snap. "He didn't say that at all."

She rounds on me. "As if I do what you tell me?" She raises her eyes heavenward. "Honest to God, it's like hanging with a bunch of Neanderthals." She looks to Beatrice. "Let's get this done so I can get out of here and take care of things myself."

The two of them walk to the private rooms, and Zack looks to me in bewilderment. We wait until the green room door shuts fast, then Zack turns to me.

"Jesus, you let her talk to you that way?"

"She isn't mine, man," I ground out. Wish to God she was. I'd have something to say about quite a few things.

"Not yours?" he asks, tipping his head to the side curiously. "And yet, you've got her holed up in your private room at a kink club. Explain that to me?"

"Like I said before, it's just to keep her safe while we investigate, okay? She was the one who came to Myers and

I made her come here because she's obviously on someone's radar."

"Right," Zack says, shaking his head. "And you two just, what? Play Rummy in that room or something?" His eyes are twinkling at me, but not for long as I play-jab him in the gut. "*Oof.* Jesus. Can dish it out but can't take it, huh? You've been giving me shit since the day we met."

"And I'll keep giving you shit until the day I die," I say. "I'm gonna fill Myers in and have her look into this place on the Cape."

Zack nods. "Let me know what you find. My folks are there, and I know the area well." He takes off to check in with Tobias in the office, and I check my email on my phone in the hopes that Myers has any news, but there's nothing. I glance at the time. I have Devin's art show at school in an hour. She'll spend the night with her mom, but I've already promised I'll go to her show. I know Devin's got some kinda recital thing she's doing later this week, and my mind is on making sure I'll have the time to get there and how I'll do it without dealing with Nichole and her drama, when I head to my room. It's been a good thirty minutes, so I figure the girls have had enough time to finish.

I slide in the key to unlock the door to my room and open it. At first, I don't see the girls, but I can hear them chattering away in the bathroom. I shut the door behind me and look around the room. I've hardly stepped foot in here in days. It looks the same, just cleaner, and it was pretty damn clean before. The floor is spotless, the windows crystal clear, not a speck of dust to be seen. Zoe's been busy. The laptop I brought her as a loan sits on a side table, and the bed is made. God, she must hate being locked up in here like this.

"Oh I don't know." I hear Zoe's voice from the open

bathroom. "It was just a one-night stand. He doesn't really have any interest in me. You warned me to stay away and I should've listened. I'm not one of you guys."

Her head is in the sink and she's tipped back, and Beatrice whips her head around to stare at me. When she catches my gaze, she narrows her eyes as if to scold me. I shrug. What the hell?

"I did warn you," Beatrice says to Zoe, but her gaze is steadily fixed on me. I give her a 'what the fuck' look because she might not be my sub, but it's still not cool to shoot daggers at me like that. "I didn't think you were into kink, and Brax lives and breathes it." She sits Zoe up and wraps her head in some sorta plastic thing. Now Zoe is looking at me, too.

"I wouldn't know," she says, unabashed. "Haven't had a chance to check it out." Bullshit. I've spanked her a few times already.

Hardly a kink show, the voice in my head says.

I blow out a breath. "You girls talking about me as if I'm not even here?" I roll my eyes heavenward and pretend to take a knife out of my chest. "Et tu, Brute?"

Beatrice helps Zoe to her feet and walks her into the room. Zoe has something draped around her shoulders to keep her clothes clean.

"Oh, stop the drama, Brax," Beatrice says, rolling her eyes at me. "Listen, this dye has to sit for thirty minutes before I can do anything, so I'm just gonna step out and catch up with Zack. He's been on a case and I haven't really seen him in a few days. That'll give *you two* a chance to catch up." She gives me a coy grin, and Zoe sticks her tongue out at her, then Beatrice leaves, the door clicking with finality. The second it does, Zoe drops all manner of civility and glares at me.

What the *fuck?*

I glance at the time. "I have to go to Devin's school. Art show night."

"Go," she says, her lips thin and tight. "I don't care if you leave now. No point in staying. I've got food and a laptop. What else could I possibly need?"

"For fuck's sake, Zoe. Jesus, you need someone to adjust that attitude for you."

And that's when I can almost see the audible snap of her resolve. Her voice is a low, slithering hiss. "What's I need is none of your fucking concern. You lost that right when you decided to spank my ass, make me come, then pretend I don't exist."

Ah. That's what this is about?

"First of all, I'm hardly pretending you don't exist," I begin, but she cuts me off with a swipe of her palm in the air.

"Save it, Braxton."

"No," I continue. "If you're so sure you know what my motives are, you have to know what's going on in my mind. I mean, how else are you supposed to make conclusions about what I'm doing?"

Her lips tighten but she doesn't try to stop me from continuing.

"You're not a member here. You're not my submissive, and you're not into any of this shit. It isn't fair of me to take advantage of you the way I did. I never should have. We had a one-night stand and it was amazing, but that's all it was. You and I both know that. You're only here because your safety matters. And that's all there is to it."

"Right," she says, her voice dripping with sarcasm. "So you've already made up your mind about what I want without asking me. That's what doms do? I wouldn't know."

What?

"No. I didn't make up your mind," I protest, feeling my own anger rising at the accusation. "I'm just saying that it isn't right for me to…"

"Take advantage," she supplies, rolling her eyes. "We've covered that."

"Have we?" Now she's got my ire up, and it takes some effort to stay calm. My palm itches to spank her little ass again, but that only gets us in trouble.

"Yeah," she says, pushing to her feet. "And let me tell you something. You didn't take advantage of me. You take advantage of people who are helpless and can't fend for themselves. And excuse me, but I think I've got that covered. Did it ever occur to you that maybe I *want* you to…" she sputters for a minute, eyes flashing, a few little damp wisps of hair sneaking underneath the plastic thing she's got on her head, "take *advantage* of me?"

I look at her curiously. "Come again?"

"Yeah, Brax," she says, rolling her eyes. "It would be *really fucking nice* to come again." I snort, but she's not laughing, so I sober up. "Dude, seriously. I'm bored to death and trying to figure out who the hell screws around with someone like me, puts them in their private room to keep them safe, and then pretends they don't exist? How does that even work?"

"Wait a minute," I say, shaking my head at her. "I don't pretend you don't exist. I've been busting my ass taking care of my kid and trying to find out what's going on with the assholes pursuing you and doing my shifts as dungeon monitor. Hardly twiddling my thumbs here, sweetheart." Was my pulling away a mistake?

She walks over to me and stabs her finger into my chest. "Don't you dare 'sweetheart' me."

"That's enough." I've had it. She's said what she has to, and I'll admit maybe my timing wasn't the best here, but

I've had enough. "You said what you had to. You carry on, and you're not gonna like where this goes."

A little of the heat quenches in her eyes as she looks at me. "Oh yeah?"

Beatrice chooses that precise moment to come in the room. She sees as at a stand-off and her eyes widen. "Did I interrupt something? I could just leave for a little while—"

"No, we're good," Zoe says. "Brax was just leaving."

She's kicking me out of my own damn room? Yeah, not happening. I smirk at her and pull a chair out. "I don't have to leave to get Devin for another fifteen minutes. I'd love to see this transformation." I sit back and fold my arms on my chest. Zoe rolls her eyes but doesn't protest as Beatrice leads her back into the bathroom and shuts the door behind them. There's the sound of water running and murmured voices, and for a minute I wonder what they're talking about.

Zoe's pissed, and honestly, it sounds as if she's got reason to be.

My phone beeps, so I slide it out of my pocket. Myers. "Yeah?"

"Got a lead. Looks like Antonia Zandetti had someone on the side."

"Lived in Cape Cod in Massachusetts?" I ask.

"Lives," he corrects.

I feel it in my gut. This is the lead we need to pursue. "Go on."

"Ted Sutherland. Former associate professor at NYCU. Widower, independently wealthy, and she studied under him for her undergrad."

"Right. Today I talked to someone who knew her as well, and it seems there's a good chance she isn't dead after all. Her body was never located, so technically she's a 'missing person,' right?"

"Exactly."

I blow out a breath. "Well I think I know where I need to pay a visit," I say.

"You going there yourself?" Myers asks.

"Hell yes I am. Need to close in on this and put shit together before something else goes down."

"Keep me posted, Cannon."

"I will." I disconnect the call as a knock sounds on the door to my room. I can hear Zack on the other side. The girls are still fussing and clanging around in the bathroom, so I go to get the door.

When I open it, Zack's standing there looking grim.

"Got confirmation from Myers that Zandetti may be with her boyfriend." Zack nods, but his eyes are grim, the lines around his lips sad. "What is it, man?"

"Car bombing, victim was an NYPD officer."

"Jesus." My stomach clenches in helpless anger. "Did he survive?"

Zack nods and sighs. "Barely. He's in the ICU but not responding. There's more, Brax. The car belonged to Zoe and her partner, Al Rumaro. Al was supposed to be off today but took the shift since Zoe isn't there. She was the one supposed to be in that car, man."

I take in a deep breath, willing myself to stay calm. That could've been Zoe. That maybe should have been.

He shakes his head. "Chief is getting concerned, but I've told him she's in good hands. He wants more intel, but we'll have to wait until we have more to give."

I hear someone clearing her throat behind us, and Zack's eyes go wide just before I turn around and see Zoe standing there looking uncharacteristically shy. Her hair is pitch black and cut short, enhancing her almond-shaped eyes and pouty lips. She looks fucking perfect, and right then, right there, something changes, and I know it isn't just because she's cute as fuck but because for just one minute, with the shade of bashfulness flushing her cheeks, I see the girl beneath the hard exterior.

A deep, abiding need to claim her thrums through me.

She's mine. She just hasn't figured that out yet.

"What do you think?" Beatrice asks.

"Don't recognize her at all," Zack admits. "Good job, babe." Beatrice beams at him, then her gaze swings around to me.

"Brax?"

I cross the room to her and give a short nod. "Perfect," I say, afraid if I say too much, I'll lose the control I have over the primal instinct to claim her and pound my chest, toss her over my shoulder and bring her to my cave. "You wanna go on a road trip?"

Her eyes widen, her voice husky when she speaks. "Leave this room? Fuck yeah."

I can't help but smile at that. "I have to go to Devin's school for an art show, but it won't take long. She goes back to her mom tonight, then you and I are heading out to the Cape. We're putting what Myers and Zack told us together, and we're hunting down Ted Sutherland, Antonia Zandetti's lover."

Her eyes are bright and excited, like she just found out we're going on vacation, not heading out to track down the pieces to the puzzle.

"Yeah I'm totally in," she says.

"Good. I'll clear my time off with Tobias and we'll keep Myers informed. Pack a bag. We leave here in ten."

I barely want to leave her for even that length of time, but I do. I debrief Tobias, then head back to the room to get her, but she's already at the door, bag slung over her shoulder. "Let's go."

Chapter 8

Zoe

HE LOOKED at me strangely when I came out with my hair all done. I'll admit Beatrice did an amazing job. She knows what she's doing. Not only did she cut my hair in a way that makes me look younger, my eyes look brighter, and my cheekbones higher, thereby changing nearly my entire appearance, but she did some magic with makeup. I felt shy going out to Brax and Zack, but I'm ready to move things along, and it had to be done. And then I looked at him… I'm not really sure what happened out there, but I felt different for a moment. Softer. Malleable.

I needed him to approve. I hate that I did, but I can't deny it. I needed him to find me pretty, to like the new haircut, and let me the fuck out of this room.

When his eyes met mine, something stirred deep within me, as if I've known him so much longer than a few days, and I knew in my gut that I *trust him. Let him take care of you,* my inner voice coaxes.

I'm not the kind of girl who lets anyone do anything for me. I survived my childhood, only to fight for what was mine as an adult. Nothing, absolutely *nothing* was handed to me, and I don't expect handouts now. Everything I have I fought for and won, and that includes my pride. But when he looks at me like that, a little part of me melts. I don't like that it does. I need to remain in control.

I toss clothes in a bag easily, as I have so little here, and meet him at the door. I'm so fucking ready to move this along. He takes the bag from my hand and slings it over his shoulder.

"I can hold that," I say, but he doesn't even bother responding, just leads the way back to Tobias's office and the exit.

"Brax," I repeat. "Give me the damn bag." The softness I felt while looking at him after I got my hair done is gone now. "I can handle it."

"No," he says, not looking at me, while we walk past the bar and through the entrance to the lobby. When we get to the main area, there's a man sitting on a bench and a woman sitting on his lap. She's got whiskers drawn on her face and little kitty ears, and she's purring against him, rubbing her cheek against his. You see all sorts of things in NYC that you don't elsewhere. Add Verge to the picture, and I'm beginning to see there really isn't a hell of a lot you won't see here. I want to see more at Verge, and I hope now that I've got this disguise going that I can move around a little more freely.

Curiosity fills me as he opens the door and we head to the street. "I parked in the parking garage down the road today," he says. "We need a little more anonymity, which is why you're not carrying this bag. Stay quiet and keep your head down."

I fucking wish someone *would* attack me. I'm ready to

take them down. I could do it with one hand tied behind me.

"I really need some way to work out at Verge," I say. "I'm going out of my mind and I need to train." I need to feel my heart pounding, my skin covered in perspiration, dotting my forehead and blurring my vision. I need the release of a punching bag and weights, pushing me to the extreme. I've been doing what I can in the cramped little room, planks and jumping jacks and running in place, but I need a lot more.

"I can work you out," he teases, smirking and making the little dimple show.

I play-punch him but he dodges it and just keeps walking with those huge steps. I keep up, but it's got me winded. He sobers then.

"Something I need to tell you," he says, but then he shakes his head. "Nah, better to tell you in the car."

"What?" He can't lead me on like that and then not saying anything. I hate when people do that.

"Wait," he orders, the playfulness gone and the dom back in place. I roll my eyes. *Whatever.*

"If you were mine, you'd learn damn quick not to roll those eyes at me," he says in a voice that resembles some sort of growl.

"Oh yeah? Good thing I'm not yours then," I say, rolling my eyes again for good measure. Son of a bitch. If I mean nothing to him, he can fuck my submission.

"You really do throw sass around like confetti," he says.

"No shit." Where the hell is this conversation going?

He shakes his head as we near the dark, dismal parking building in front of us. "Behave yourself around my daughter. I don't care who the hell you are, you watch your language and keep it clean."

"Excuse me? Who do you think I am? Jesus. I know how to behave around kids."

He opens the door for me and narrows his eyes as we go through. "Sometimes I wonder," is all he says. "When she's gone, you and I need to lay shit on the line. For now, just behave yourself."

No one, literally *no one* pisses me off like this man. It's annoying as hell he doesn't think I have the self-respect to contain myself in front of his kid.

"Fuck you," I say. "Let me in the damn car and stop the lecture, grandpa. I've got it under control."

"The hell you do," he says, as he slams open the passenger door to a sleek silver sedan. I slide in the passenger seat, still fuming, and he tosses the bag in the back before he slides in next to me.

"We're in the car now," I say. "Tell me what it is you wanted to tell me."

"In a minute."

Control freak of America, that's what he is. Leave it to me to land myself an absolute control freak. Honest to fucking God.

Sighing, I lean back against the seat. If we keep snapping at each other like this, it's gonna be one fucking long road trip.

He pays for parking at the exit and pulls out of the lot, driving slowly as we're in typical mid-afternoon gridlock.

"We don't have far to go," he says. "But we have enough time to talk. First, Al Rumaro was involved in an accident today."

I don't know what I expected him to tell me, but this isn't it.

Oh God.

"Yeah?" I ask, my mouth dry.

He nods. "Yeah."

"Is he okay?" I ask.

He nods. "Zack says he's in the ICU and unresponsive, but he's alive."

Unresponsive? Still alive isn't always a blessing in these cases. *God.*

"Was he driving?"

"Listen, Zoe. He was in a car you were supposed to be in," he says. "And the car was rigged with a bomb. So it doesn't take a rocket scientist to figure this one out."

I nod, my mouth dry. "Yeah," I manage to croak out. "Jesus, Braxton. We need to find out who the hell is behind this and do something about it."

"We do." We drive in silence, crawling along the congested streets, before he speaks up again. "And you know it'll be a helluva lot easier if you stop fighting me."

What the fuck? I turn to look at him, incredulous. "Now *wait* a minute. Dude, I'm not the one fighting here. You're the one who had the fucking gall to spank me, fuck me, then leave me for days on end."

He blows out a breath. "I didn't leave you. I've been at Verge every single day looking in on you."

Oh no, he is not playing dumbass with me. "That's not what I mean, and you fucking know it."

"Damn truck driver mouth," he mutters, but I ignore him and continue.

"You don't talk to me. You barely come in the room. What kind of an asshole has that kind of intimacy with someone and then just leaves them? Tell me, Braxton. Is that like a dom thing?"

He growls, flicks his directional, and takes a left at the light.

"Listen, I already told you, I didn't want to take advantage of you. I mean, Jesus. Look at this situation. You're being pursued by someone who wants to fucking kill you.

You get involved with me, and that only makes you even more conspicuous."

I blow out a breath. "I didn't say I want to get involved. Jesus!"

Frowning, he pulls up to an intersection with parents and children crossing the street. Looks like we've arrived. "Then what *do* you want, Zoe?"

I shake my head. I really don't know how to answer that question.

He parks the car and looks at me, waiting. "I don't know Brax. I really don't. I just know you piss me off."

"Likewise," he says, and briefly his eyes twinkle.

"Maybe this would be different under different circumstances," I tell him.

"Maybe," he agrees with a shrug. He cuts the engine and looks back to me. "Remember what I said. Best behavior. You so much as swear, and you'll answer to me."

Even though his bossiness makes me mad, I can't help but admit my heart flutters a bit in my chest at his dominance. It's been three fucking days since he's touched me, and my body responds of its own accord.

"What does that mean?" I want to know. Hell, I *need* to know. "What does that fucking even *mean?*" Who the hell is he that he just issues threats like that?

He drops the keys on the console, and something in him seems to snap. Before I know what's happening, his hands are wound in my short hair and he's tugging my head closer to his mouth, his lips brushing mine, but when we touch it's like a match set to kindling. Flames lick at my core, he groans into my mouth, and he deepens the kiss, a firmer press of his lips on mine. The kiss takes my breath away in its vehemence and heat, then it's over way too fast. "I'll tell you what that means," he growls in my ear, and he's so damn serious his eyes are pools of flames, his voice as deep and raspy as I've ever heard it. "You behave yourself around my kid, or tonight when I have you alone, you'll find your pants around your ankles, and you'll be belly-down over my knee. I'll paint your ass red and punish you. Is that clear enough?"

I nod, my heart thundering in my chest. "You can't go around issuing spanking threats to me," I protest.

"Then I'd better make good on the promise," he says, raising a brow.

"Yeah?" I say, needing to push him. "I'll believe it when I see it."

God. I *am* baiting him.

But whatever. "I'll watch my mouth and behave myself and I won't embarrass you. Good enough?"

"First of all," he says. "This has shit all to do with you embarrassing me. I'm raising a kid in NYC. I fight to keep her innocence, and you're not gonna screw that up."

It's both sweet and maddening, and I'm not sure what to think. On the one hand, I love that he fights to keep his little girl innocent. On the other, who the hell does he think he is implying I'd do anything to threaten that?

"Second of all, I've had it with you baiting me." Though his eyes simmer, his voice is controlled and he's deadly serious. "We'll check into a hotel tonight, and you're going over my lap."

"Thank fucking God." He blinks in surprise, and I'm not even sure why I said it myself. This whole week has been a mash of confusion and I don't know what end is up.

He shakes his head, the anger dissipating as his lips quirk up. "You confuse the hell out of me," he mutters.

"I confuse the hell out of myself," I mutter. I know when he's being that stern dom he's with me and not checked out. There's something different about me, too.

It's baffling but intuitively I know I relate to him on that level.

He smiles at me, reaches for my hand, and squeezes. "Come on, baby. Let's go. I want you to meet my little girl."

There he is. That sweet, dominant man who makes me feel like myself for a little while. I wish I could make him stay this time.

He leads me into the brick building, his chin lifted in pride and that makes me hold my head higher. He's happy to have me with him and he's taking me to see his little girl. This means something.

The familiar smell of books and chalk and graham crackers, or whatever it is that makes an elementary school smell like one, fills my senses. I hate schools. I'm unprepared for the way just the smell alone, decades later, fucks with my head. Drawings of sunsets and green trees with vivid red apples, drawn crudely in crayon, line the walls, hung haphazardly like a helper who couldn't quite reach high enough did the job.

A dented locker catches my attention and I shut my eyes as a memory floods me, drowning me, without warning.

"You think because your guardian is wealthy you mean something, don't you?" The cruel twist of Mrs. Lapis' lips makes my tummy hurt. She hates me. She saw when I pulled Carolyn, her little pet's hair, during recess. She didn't hear the way Carolyn mocked the fact that I'm wearing a long-sleeved t-shirt in June, but I have to, to hide the bruises. No one can know.

"You mean nothing to him. You're a name on paper".

I stare at the dented locker, wishing I could hide inside it, to hide from her and Carolyn and the evil man who gave me the bruises…

The memory fades at the tug on my arm. I blink,

surprised that I'm in a full hallway, not the vacant one with the cruel teacher.

"Zoe?" Brax is looking down at me, his brows furrowed in concern. "Where'd you go there?"

I open my mouth to say something, to hide what happened because I have no idea how to tell him what just happened, but a squealed "Daddy!" interrupts us. A blonde-haired, blue-eyed girl with two braids bouncing on either side of her launches herself at him. The sight of him bending down and scooping her into his arms warms me, and when he kisses the top of her head, I melt. She's slight, with a smattering of freckles on her nose, and she smiles with curiosity when she sees me.

"Devin, this is Zoe."

"You have a girlfriend?" she asks, tipping her head to the side.

Brax looks me over and winks. "No, honey, just a friend." I temper an eye-roll. Friends spank each other and fuck each other all the time, I guess, in his world. The idea makes me smirk. But I know he has a crazy ex, and it's likely safer for us not to be paired as "boyfriend/girlfriend," especially by a little girl who may not know discretion.

"Zoe, you can come see my art show," Devin says, taking my hand. I haven't held a little hand like this in… ever? She takes Brax's hand in hers, and it feels nice having her between us like this. I could get used to this, I think, but the thought passes briefly. Just the fact that Brax has a little girl makes him off limits to me. I'm not the kind of person that handles the whole motherhood thing. I'd be a terrible mother, I know it, I'm way too temperamental.

"What do you have on display here tonight, kiddo?" Brax asks, his normally husky voice softer than I've heard yet.

"I painted water lilies," she says. "And a moon with stars, a field of daisies, sunflowers, and roses, and a little girl with a pony."

Brax's lips twitch up. "One of these things is not like the other," he chants.

Devin grins, then leads us into a classroom that's filled with people, parents and children and paintings galore lining the walls. An older woman with glasses and graying hair pinned to her nape looks over the room with a smile of benevolence. I guess that's her teacher.

"So nice to meet you, Mr. Cannon," she says with a smile. "And you, too, Mrs. Cannon."

"Oh," I stammer. "I'm just a family friend. I'm not Mrs. Cannon." I feel a bit of a pang. I don't belong here. I'm an intruder.

"Oh, I'm so sorry," she says. "I haven't met Devin's mother yet and made assumptions." I give a half-hearted shrug but I'm a little taken aback. This is NYC, for crying out loud. It's not at all uncommon for someone to have an unconventional family structure. But then I realize something that makes me a little sad. She mistook me for Devin's mom because Devin's mom hasn't shown up.

I might not be the best mother if I were one, but if I had a kid, you'd bet your ass I'd meet their teachers, even if I had to have someone cover my shifts or I had to make a special appointment. I guess some people can't always make it because of work, but it would surprise me if that's why Devin's mom couldn't come. Brax doesn't have Devin in the evenings, and if she had a babysitter, she wouldn't have called him to get her early the other day.

I shake my head. This is none of my business. The teacher is chattering away to Brax, who's listening with interest, and leads us over to the artwork that lines the wall. The work is childlike but pretty, with vibrant colors and bold line strokes. I muse as I look at it. When do people learn to be timid? When do they learn that it's not okay to be who you want to be? I look at Devin's carefree face and know she hasn't hit that point yet. I hope she never does.

"What do you think, daddy?" Devin asks, reaching for Braxton's hand. She tugs him over to the boldest, a blue night sky with brilliant gold stars.

He towers over everyone in this room with his tall frame and has to bend down a little to look. He peers at is as if we're perusing the halls of the Metropolitan Museum of Art and strokes his chin. "I think it reminds me of something I've seen before by someone who was an *impressionist.*"

"Starry Night?" I supply helpfully.

He snaps his fingers and his eyes twinkle at me. "Yes. Exactly."

Devin just looks at him soberly. "You think, daddy? You like it? Then you can have it when we're done. We get to take our art home and I want this one on your fridge. Your fridge is too boring anyway."

Brax chuckles. "Oh yeah? Your job to brighten it up? I'd love that. You know I left it boring on purpose just so I could decorate it with something you made."

She smiles, her eyes meeting his with pride, and she looks tickled. "Well then it's a deal." She sticks her hand out to shake. God, she's adorable. Soberly, he takes her hand and shakes firmly.

"I'll hold you to that," he says in his growly voice, making her smile.

"Can we get cookies now?" Her brows draw together, and she lifts her eyes to his expectantly.

"Cookies?"

"The sign says refreshments served after," I supply, pointing to the doorway.

He looks over to where I'm pointing, takes a step to me and mutters, "We don't have a lot of time. We have to get on the road."

I shrug. "I think it'll make your girl happy."

He frowns. "Yeah. I think I'm just on edge since Nichole is due any minute. She's just gonna be nasty when she meets you."

"I thought you said she has a man?"

"She's had several. Doesn't mean she doesn't turn into the Wicked Witch of the West when *I* bring one around."

"Double standard?"

"Totally."

I grin at him and whisper so Devin doesn't hear. "Oh let me at her."

He grins back and replies to Devin, but his eyes are on me. "Of course we'll get refreshments, baby. Lead the way."

Devin pulls his hand and expertly weaves her way in and out of the crowds until she reaches the door, then shows us how to get to the library, chattering the whole way. As we walk, my mind is playing tricks on me. I remember oh so much as I'm assaulted by one familiar smell after another. Books and crayons and backpacks and glue, cardboard and sneakers and little children all pressed together before recess. I haven't given much headspace to my childhood in years, and it's a veritable memory bath as we go there. As before, Devin takes one of my hands and one of Brax's, and we walk together. Irrationally, I wish he was holding my hand instead. I don't like how I feel being here.

When we enter the library, Devin makes a beeline for the refreshment table. It's been set up along one wall, with cookies and juice, a large thermal coffee maker, and little white plates and napkins. It looks so tranquil that I almost forget the way I was bullied in a library, the way my foster father, the principal of the school I attended, would take me to the school library when he wanted to upbraid me for getting in trouble. I close my eyes and will myself not to remember being shoved in the stock room closet, slapped against the cluster of shelves in the way back, with a promise of misery when he got me home alone.

For a moment, I'm struck with the incongruity of everything. We're hunting down murderers, closing in on the names and whereabouts of people who've done unspeakable crimes, and yet here we stand in the most innocent of places, drinking watered-down schoolhouse coffee and eating chocolate chip cookies off napkins while surrounded by large cardboard cut-outs that line the walls with words like *Feed your Brain: Read.*

There's one more cookie on a plate and Devin snatches it up. I wonder if the cookie ever touches her lips, as she devours the cookie. "Easy, now," Brax chides, his eyes narrowed on her. "Have you had your dinner?"

She shakes her head. He crosses his arms on his chest. "Why haven't you? You didn't tell me that. You know you're not allowed cookies if you haven't had your dinner."

My heart thumps a little hearing him. He's a good daddy.

She scowls.

"Devin," he warns.

"Mom made broccoli soup," she says with a frown. "It didn't even have cheese or anything. It was just like lumps of broccoli and it was *gross*. I hardly like eating a tiny bite of broccoli mom makes me when she makes it as a side dish. Eating it in soup is disgusting."

Brax's lips twitch, but before he can respond, a sharp, high-pitched voice interrupts.

"It was not disgusting, and you could've found that

out for yourself if you'd tried it." I turn in the direction of the voice, and I'm momentarily speechless. Damn. He didn't prepare me for how beautiful Nichole is. She has the same platinum blonde hair as her daughter. It swings down her back in a long sheet, thick and full. Her eyes are wide, framed with thick lashes, and her makeup is impeccable. She has high cheekbones flushed pink, full red lips, and a knockout figure. She holds the hand of a man who stands silent, a brooding, handsome guy with dark hair and eyes.

"Nice to see you, Nichole," Brax says, his arms crossed on his chest. "Someone I should meet?"

Nichole rolls her eyes. "This is my boyfriend Reggie," she says. "And who's *this?*"

Well that didn't take her long. Damnit, I like her kid, but I already want to tell Nichole to kiss my ass. What the hell was Brax thinking hooking up with her?

Before Brax can say anything, I stick out my hand. "Zoe," I say, not offering anything else.

She frowns at my hand and keeps her hands on her hips. "Nice to meet you," she says, turning away. "Brax, are you taking Devin tonight?"

Brax blows out a breath with practiced patience, his eyes flaming. Jesus, he's intimidating when he's angry. I've seen him angry before, but I wouldn't want to be on the receiving end of the heat I feel now. I make a mental note to myself never to cross him, and weirdly, I'm a little attracted to the way his jaw tightens and his arms tense when he crosses them on his chest.

"We talked about this, Nichole," he says. "I can't tonight. It isn't my night, so I haven't prepared, and I have an important errand to run."

She purses her lips and gives him a sickly-sweet smile. "Oh, that's right. Since she isn't yours full-time, you have to *plan* to take her, unlike the rest of us who just parent every day."

His eyes grow impossibly more heated. "Don't go there," he says in a low hiss. While other people wander around, laughing and joking, the tension between them grows, and a line of worry forms in Devin's brows. I feel for her caught in the middle of this. I never had parents to fight over me, but I have been the kid at a school night without happy parents by her side, so I know she just wants things to be okay. I scoot my way over to her. I don't need to get involved in their little spat anyway.

"Show me your favorite section in the library?" I ask her with a smile. "What do you like best?"

"Dog stories," she says with a grin, grabbing my hand and pulling me over to a display of picture books with all sorts of puppies and dogs on the covers. I want to get out of here. I can feel the oppressive heat of being in a school like this closing in on me, and I'm pissed at myself for being weak and stupid. I also want to be alone with Brax. I want to know what the fuck is going on with us, and we need to get moving to close in on our next lead, but Devin's more important than what I want right now. I'd be a crappy mother, but I know enough.

Just as Devin pulls a book off a shelf and hands it to me, I hear a hissed voice near my ear. "Oh no, you don't. You don't get to come in here and play mom on me and try to take over. No *way*." I blink up at Nichole's furious eyes. She may be beautiful, but she looks part-terrier with her eyes all narrowed like that.

"Excuse me?" I pull myself to my full height, which isn't much but at least I'm not cowering to her. I'm not gonna cause a scene, but there's no way I'll let her tear me down. I might not be totally on my game here, but I'm no pushover. And Devin might be her kid, but she's Brax's, too, and he's with me.

"I said you don't get to play mom," she growls, moving closer to me. God, what I wouldn't do to level her right now. She's as skinny as a twig and I can tell by the aggressive stance she holds; the girl doesn't know anything about a real throw down. I imagine how easily it would be to floor her: smack her chest with an open-palm slap, watch her stumble, then sweep her legs. I'm not a violent person but I'm no pacifist, and my protective instincts do come into play when a child is on the line.

I give her a smile that says, "Back off, bitch," and take a step toward her. "I'm not playing anything. While you two were having your little fight, I asked Devin to show me her favorite books. If you have a problem with that, maybe you should've shown up earlier so you could stake your claim." Stoking her anger is stupid, but I can't seem to help myself.

"Zoe." Brax's warning tone sounds behind me, but I ignore him.

"Her teacher didn't even know I wasn't her mom," I say, watching as the anger fades to something else and Nichole takes a step back. "Not sure why that is, Nichole, but if I were you, I'd do something about that."

"*Zoe.*" I look at Brax. He's shaking his head from side to side, quietly instructing me to back the hell down. I don't want to, but I know he's right. I won't stoop to the level of causing a scene like these two did. I give her a smile and turn to go.

"I see how it is," she says, following behind me with a chuckle. She speaks low enough so only I hear her. "He tells you to jump and you say 'how high?' So you play his sick, perverted games. That's why he's brought you here, so he can demonstrate he finally brought a woman to heel."

Bring me to *heel?* Is that a thing? I want to slap the smug look off her face, and Brax and I are gonna have a talk about these "perverted ways," but I keep my head about me and instead turn to Devin, who's still looking at the books and thankfully oblivious to what's gone on between me and her mom. "Devin?" I say, taking control by ignoring Nichole entirely. "It was a pleasure to meet you. Your dad and I need to get going, now, but I fully plan on being with him the next time you're with him, and I'd love to read some of these books together. Sound good?"

Devin grins at me and gives me a little wave. Nichole watches in silence, and Brax stands behind, taking it all in and not missing a damn detail.

"We'll talk later, Nichole," he says, then walks over to Devin and picks her up in a bear hug so fierce he lifts her straight off the floor. She squeals, and my insides melt. Watching the two of them makes something wistful blossom inside me. My heart feels softer toward him, and I can forgive the way he's ignored me when I see with my own eyes why. I like seeing this big bear of a man swooning over his little girl. I've only just met her, but I like her.

She's his. How could I not?

He comes up to me and takes me by the hand, pulling me too close for it to be polite, and he hisses in my ear. "You do not rise to her bait. Just keep walking. I'll keep her away from you and won't let you near her venom, but for Christ's sake, don't poke her."

"Yes, sir," I say with biting sarcasm. "Since you've taken me to heel I suppose that's the right response."

His only reply is a low growl and a firmer grasp on my hand. We march down the hallway and toward the street, and I realize I'm holding my breath. Devin and Nichole distracted me for a bit but now I'm feeling the walls close in on me again. It's fucked up, but I need to get out of here. The hallway seems hot, the heat oppressive, pushing on my chest like a too-thick blanket, muffling my ability to breathe deeply. I focus on the click-clack of our shoes on the linoleum and breathe through my mouth so I don't have to inhale the smell of the school that makes me sick.

I'm anxious and hate this.

I'm fine meeting the teacher and the kid. And cookies and facing off against the she bitch. Now I'm freaking out.

"Zoe." Brax's voice seems distant and hollow.

"Mmm," I respond, keeping my lips pressed tight so I don't make a fool of myself in front of everyone, keeping the nausea at bay by focusing on the doorway. This is utter bullshit. Last year I landed myself in a drug cartel sting that was so highly charged, I thought my partner was gonna wet his pants. I was the one that led it, I was the one who brought down the ringleader and held him at gunpoint while my fellow officers cuffed and apprehended the suspects. And now all I've done is confronted his bitchy ex *in a school* and I can hardly keep my shit together?

I tug my hand away from him and smack open the door to the school so hard it creaks on its hinges. I grab it as it swings back, welcoming the smack on my hand with the force of its return. The sharp hit on my palm grounds me somehow, clears my brain, and when I get outside I take in huge lungfuls of air as if I've just surfaced from being underwater. My head swims. Instinctively I step to the side, bend my knees, and rest my elbows on my knees, breathing in deep.

"Zoe. Jesus, Zoe." Braxton is right next to me, reaching for me, but I push him away. I hardly want anyone to see me, let alone touch me.

"Hey, you alright?" The breath fills my lungs and my vision clears, blood rushing to my head. I inhale and exhale, then venture to lift my head and look at him.

"Sorry about that," I whisper, shaking my head and looking away so I don't need to read the concern in his eyes. "I don't know what happened." It's not exactly a lie. I suspect I know what happened, but I can't focus on the whys right now.

He watches me with concern, his lips pulled tight, his strong jaw clenched. Is he angry with me? I take in another breath. "I'm fine," I insist.

"Is it because of what she said?" he asks, frowning.

I snort out a laugh. "About bringing me to heel? Clearly, she doesn't know me very well if she thinks you've done *that*. I might not be up on the lingo, but even I'm smart enough to know what the implication is there."

His stern features soften, and the dimple dots his cheek with his smile. "Damn right about that," he mutters. "Would take a man with cast iron balls to bring you to heel, and even then, you'd likely cut them off."

I laugh out loud, shaking my head. "Yeah, whatever," I say, but a part of me is a little sad. I think I might like some of this submission thing. I definitely like the dominance thing. Don't they go hand in hand? But now's not the time to talk about it. We've got way, way bigger fish to fry.

"Let's go," he says, extending his hand out to me. But he doesn't take mine this time. He waits for me to take his.

This conversation isn't over. I know that and I'm guessing so does he, but we have time to figure this out. I take his hand and we walk like that to the car. We've got a long ride ahead of us.

Chapter 9

Braxton

She's sleeping quietly next to me, soft, whiffling snores making me smile to myself. She's got her arms tucked under her like a little girl. Is she cold? I reach out and gently brush my finger on her arm, but she's warm. Still, I flick on the heat and put it up just a notch. I want her comfortable. I like that she's relaxed enough to rest like this.

We've almost arrived. The drive took five hours, including our stop for dinner at a roadside diner. I think the burger and fries did her good and she relaxed into a nap afterward. The pale pallor of her face after leaving the school has lessened, and the familiar pink flush is back. I'm glad. I hated that look on her face.

We have a lot to talk about.

On the way here, we talked as if we'd known each other for years. We talked about bands we liked, movies we'd seen, classes we took in college, our favorite places to vacation and our favorite ways to pass the time. We talked about clothes and shoes and cars and limos, rock bands and pop bands and grunge bands, where we've traveled to and where we'd like to go. She's easy to talk to, and even has a sense of humor when she doesn't feel threatened. She made me laugh so hard recounting a road trip she took with friends in college that I was wiping tears away by the time she was done. But there was plenty we didn't talk about.

Her past. Mine. Kinky things that pique her curiosity at the club.

Us.

I pull off the Bourne Bridge, only a mile away from the little hotel I booked. Cape Cod is a small, coastal area south of Boston, a little cape that juts out into the Atlantic.

"Hey, sleeping beauty." I gently nudge her, smiling to myself when I remember how hard she can be to wake up. She grunts and rolls over, the seatbelt leaving a red mark against her chest. "Zoe. Almost at the hotel, babe." Still, nothing. I poke her again, shaking her shoulder, keeping an eye on the GPS, and my voice gets deeper. "Hey. *Zoe*. Wake up. We're almost there." I marvel to myself that she can sleep as well here as she can in bed. I mean, we're in a freaking car. It's a little annoying, though, when you need to get someone moving. I shake her shoulder again, earning me a grunt. She mumbles something incoherent. I take the final turn to the hotel, then when I'm driving straight again I reach over and give her ass a sharp slap.

"Hey!" she bolts upright. "Dude, that's so not even fair." She adorably rubs her ass and frowns at me.

"Like waking the fucking dead," I mutter. "Gonna start waking you with a riding crop."

She glares.

"What? It'll work better than a bugle," I muse.

She looks out the window, and though it's dark out, the streets are lined with streetlights that still cast a glow on the old-fashioned sidewalks outside quaint mom and pop stores that are dark now that they're closed but illuminated enough we can see the hand-tooled signs for ice cream, shoes, and a hardware store.

"Wow," she breathes. "This is cute."

"You haven't seen anything yet," I say to her with pride, as if I own this place. It is one of my favorite places to go, though. "Tomorrow, I'll take you to the beach."

"That's not why we're here, though," she says quietly.

"I know. But it doesn't mean we can't see a little while we're here."

She nods and rubs the heels of her hands into her eyes, yawning widely. "How long was I asleep?" she asks on a yawn. I take the turn into the winding drive that brings us to our hotel.

"About an hour. Feel any better?"

"No. I feel exhausted," she says with a laugh.

"Well let's get you to bed, then." I park the car and go around to open the door for her. She steps out and stretches, lifting her arms straight up in the air with an adorable yawn. I can't help but lean in and hug her, before bending down to brush my lips over hers. As if surprised, her arms reach around for me tentatively, then with more confidence, before her mouth parts and she welcomes the kiss. Too soon, we pull away.

"What was that for?" she whispers.

"You just looked pretty," I say, releasing her so I can grab our bags. A few minutes later, we're checked into our room, taking the elevator to the top floor. It's got a small but well-furnished lobby, and its well past quiet hour so it feels like we have the place to ourselves. I slide the key in the slot, open the door, and usher her in. The door shuts with a click behind us.

Immediately, she kicks off her shoes and face plants

into the bed. I toss the bags next to the wall, kick off my shoes, and join her in bed, kneeling with my knees on either side of her. I bend down and whisper in her ear. "Don't you think you ought to take these clothes off?"

"So tired," she mutters. "Do I really need to?"

I give her a playful smack on the ass. "I can help you," I offer. I lift my knee so I'm on the other side of her and can now tug off her top, followed by her leggings. She wriggles a little to help me but is otherwise dead weight on the bed.

"You really are wiped," I say with mock regret, reaching for the latch on her bra. "It's too bad I promised you a spanking when we got here."

Her eyes still closed, one corner of her lips quirks up. "That can wait for the morning," she says, but her voice holds a note of hope.

I reach for the elastic on her panties and drag them down over the curve of her gorgeous, rounded ass. "I don't think so, baby."

She doesn't protest as I pull her panties down her thighs, over her knees, then gently over each of her feet so now she lies naked on the bed in front of me. I toss them on the floor with the rest of her clothes, then join her back on the bed, leaning on one elbow, so I can take in her curves that are on full display. I run one hand along the swell of her ass, then down to her thighs with firm strokes, as if massaging the skin awake. I love the feel of her soft, sensual skin beneath my hand, satiny smooth and creamy white.

I'll fix that.

Not yet, though.

As I massage her gently, kneading her skin with soft, firm strokes of my fingers and palms, she sighs softly.

"Thought you were asleep," I tease, moving my hands back to her ass.

"Mmm." She makes a noncommittal sound. I push her thighs apart and run my hands down her inner thighs in slow, circular motions, letting the sides of my hands just graze the sweet spot between her legs before moving downward. She tenses as I draw my hands up her thighs again, her breath hitching. I smirk to myself, moving my hands up and watching as the closer I get to her pussy, the more she tenses.

"You need me to touch you there?" I tease, drawing my fingertip up the center of her leg, tracing around the underside of her ass, then down again between her thighs.

"Mmm," she says again. Without warning, I lift my hand and slap her ass again.

"Ow!" she protests.

Well, that's better than "mmm."

My dick tightens in my pants at the sight of my red handprint painting her ass.

"Told you you were getting a spanking tonight," I say with a hint of warning in my voice just before I slap her ass again. To my surprise, she pushes up on her elbows, lays her chest flat on the bed, and arches her back, gifting her naked ass to me.

"That's a good girl," I approve, positioning myself to one side so I can hold her firmly under my hand, before I spank her again, taking time in between each stroke of my palm to fondle her, to slide my hands down her breasts and to her nipples, back to her ass, then down between her soft, sweet folds. "You need this."

Her breath hitches and her eyes stay closed, but she tenses now, waiting for my palm. I spank her again and again, my hand branding her every time my palm connects with her skin, building a heated rhythm so that I can feel the heat emanating from her now-reddened skin. I kneel behind her, but she wiggles her ass in protest. I know that sign well. She needs more.

I push myself off the bed and reach for my belt buckle. At the sound of the jiggling, her eyes fly open and her mouth parts in silent protest.

"Don't worry, Zoe. I've got you. I won't give you more than you can handle." Fear and apprehension blossom in her gaze as she watches me swish the belt through the loops and wrap it around my hand, tucking the buckle in my palm so I have a strap. She should be a little afraid. That's part of the whole experience.

"Well, *now* I'm awake," she mutters. I grin at her. So fucking sweet.

"Good girl," I say. "Keep your chest down, Zoe. If you get up too quickly I could hit the wrong place." Belts are flexible, and my aim has to be just right. I want to paint that ass red. A few lashes to her thighs will hurt, but if I do it just right, she'll like it. Tomorrow, we'll investigate what we need to, and spend some time together, but tonight, we need to reconnect, and what she said earlier leads me to believe this is the way we need to begin.

"Ass up." My voice takes on a grittier, dominating edge. I can almost taste how good it will feel, and I'm already hard. I stand behind her, snap the belt on my thigh for a quick check, and watch as she jumps just a little, then melts back onto the bed. Slowly, her fingers grip onto the bedspread and clench, her knuckles turning white.

"Sometimes it helps to be reminded who's in charge, babygirl." It's my only warning before I bring back the belt and snap it on her perfect ass. She arches, her chest heaving forward, and she makes a little mewling noise.

"Back in position," I order. Like a good little girl, she listens. I spank her again, watching in pleasure how the lash leaves a red line across her ass. Like an artist painting a canvas, I lay a second, then third stripe. She's humming softly, somewhere between a moan and a whimper. She's taken her first stripes bravely. I lean over and run my hand over the slightly raised marks. I haven't spanked her hard enough to welt badly, but she's new and will likely bruise. Leather burns, then fades to warmth, and I feel it's the most erotic implement I own.

"You hanging in there?" I ask her. We haven't talked about consent or safewords or any of the trappings of consensual BDSM yet.

"Yes," she says, her voice low and husky, and I can tell just from her tone she wants more. Maybe even *needs* more.

"If this gets to be too much, you need a safeword."

"Vanilla."

I huff out a laugh. She's chosen a hell of a safeword.

"Vanilla?"

"Yup."

She doesn't even need to ask me what a safeword is. Someone's been doing her homework.

"Got it." I move back and let the lash fly once more. She hisses and arches with each strike of the belt, but the time between arching and presenting again for the next stripe lessens. She's warming into this. With every smack of my belt, I'm taking her deeper into a place she needs to be, the place where she trusts me to lead her. Where she'll let go of what's on her mind, lost in the power of sensation. Every stinging lash will clear her mind, as the push and pull of pain then pleasure releases endorphins into her body.

Some women like to be fucked to forget what bothers them. Zoe favors drink. I'll give her the taste of something better.

Rearing back, I spank her harder this time, a welt rising

on her skin, but she barely flinches. I place the belt on the bed and take a moment to massage her reddened, striped skin, applying gentle pressure that will reduce bruising. She'll mark from this, but most submissives like a little mark anyway.

I take my position behind her, drunk on wielding power over such a strong, powerful woman. She's the one who gives me control. She's the one that chooses to trust me. My dick's so hard it's painful, but I stay in control behind her. She needs more, and I'm happy to be the one to give this to her. The slow, steady thrum of leather striking bare skin fills the room, her moans softer now, when I finally decide she's had enough. I lean down, gathering her short, silky black hair between my fingers and tugging her head to the side. I lean down and brush my lips along her temple. Her lips quirk up in a smile, her eyes closed tight.

"You liked your spanking," I whisper against the shell of her ear. "You took it like such a good girl. If I touch your pretty little pussy, will I find it wet and wanting?"

She nods eagerly. "Yes," she whispers.

I reach for her hair and give a gentle but firm tug. "That's yes, sir."

Her features tighten just a bit, her eyes still closed but her lips ever so slightly thinned. "Yes, sir," she whispers, then her whole countenance softens as she welcomes this new change.

Yes, sir.

What this girl gives me is priceless.

I tug her head back again and watch as her mouth parts open in pleasure. I bend down and run my tongue along her neck, tasting the sweet, salty skin, then I kiss her. Her pulse beneath my lips pounds steady, her body tense with lust and anticipation. Still holding her hair firmly in my left hand, I shift so I can dip my fingers between her thighs. As before, I stroke the tender skin between her legs but don't go any further. This time, her thighs are painted with her desire. Her legs spread so far, the sweet, heady smell of feminine arousal hits my senses. I groan, unable to tease her any longer, and plunge my fingers where she wants them.

"Fuck yeah, that's a good girl," I groan. "Such a sweet, wet pussy. Someone likes my belt." Two fingers deep, I work her hard. "Getting you to behave will be hopeless," I say, a wicked grin tipping my lips up. "Someone likes her whippings too much."

She hums with need, her lips parted. "Yes, sir," she moans, her back arching, legs spread further apart.

"You're perfect," I groan, releasing her just long enough to reach into my wallet for a condom. She whimpers when she loses my touch.

She nods, tugging against my hold, and a shiver courses through her. Mouth slightly parted, I watch as her grasp on the bedspread tightens.

"Fuck me," she grinds out in a hoarse whisper. "Please Brax."

I let her hair go and spank her naked ass.

"Sir! Please, sir."

"Good girl," I whisper, releasing her hair and lining up behind her. "Say it. Say *this pussy is yours. It belongs to you.*"

Her words jumble in a haze of lust, pleading. She's near incoherent with want. "This pussy's yours," she says, then lets out a moan as I enter her with a savage trust. A half-sob colors her next sentence. "It—it—belongs—to *youuuu.*"

"Fuck yes it does." I plunge into her, hard, claiming what's mine, claiming what she grants me.

"Mine," I say with another hard thrust. "Mine," I

repeat, her hot ass against my skin. *"Mine."* I reach for her breasts and palm them harshly, tweaking her nipples with punishing clamps of my fingers. "Come, Zoe. Let go."

She shatters her release as I chase my own orgasm, a wordless, brutal melding of bliss and groans. I fall beside her, our bodies still entwined. I lower my mouth to the tattoo on her shoulder and give her the softest kiss. The savage within me now put to rest, I'm consumed with the primal need to take care of her. I withdraw from her and reach to the side of the bed to grab my t-shirt to clean her up. The worry lines between her eyes are gone, a look of utter peace on her face, her eyes closed.

"I needed that, Braxton," she whispers. One eye opens. "Sir?" She looks shy saying that to me now.

I lean down and kiss her cheek. "I know you did, baby-girl. I did, too." I don't punish her for calling me by name now. There will be times when she needs me to be her sir, and times when she needs me her equal.

I make my way to the bathroom and clean up, then instruct her to do the same. I can see the how fatigued she is, her whole body slumps against the ivory sink as she taps her toothbrush and sets it down.

"Come here, baby." I open up my arms behind her and she turns to me, lifting her arms like a little girl. I tuck her into my chest, welcoming the tight grip, and just let her burrow into me. During the light of day, she won't let me see that she needs to be held. When she's stripped down and sated, I'll show her she can trust me. Hell, I need to hold her. Without another word, I release her, bend down, and lift her up against my chest. Her head falls to my shoulder, and she releases a soft sigh. She's as supple as I've ever seen her, quiet and subdued. At peace, even. I've torn down her walls and she now knows that she can trust me.

"Let's get you to bed." My voice is strangely husky in the quiet room. With long strides, I bring her to bed and lay her on the mattress. Something shifted in her tonight. Or was it today? She rests her head on the pillow, and I lift the crumpled blanket, smoothing it over her, then join her in bed.

Her eyes no longer look tired, and when I lay down beside her, she looks up at me with curiosity. "What other kinky things do you like?" she whispers. "I think we've got spanking covered. You said bondage?"

I didn't expect her to be chatty, so I think for a moment before replying. "I like bondage," I say. "It's sexy, and I like the control."

"Shocking," she says with a giggle, tucking her hands under her chin. I love the snarky Zoe but having her here like this, soft and sweet, without the defensive edge she normally has, I can't help but wonder how I'll keep her here. I reach out and tuck a wisp of hair behind her ear, then gently stroke her head, letting my fingers rake through the soft black hair.

"You can be very gentle for a big, scary dom," she whispers, her lips tipping up into a barely-there smile.

"Big, scary dom?" I ask with a grin. We're so close I can smell her faintly floral scent and hear the soft whisper of her breath on the pillow. I picked a quaint little hotel, with excellent reviews, and I'm glad I did. It's cozy and warm in here, and she looks so pretty with the ivory, embroidered pillowcase behind her head.

"Mhm," she breathes. "You just spanked me with your belt, dude."

I shrug. "True." And I'd do it again if I needed to. I'd do it again if *she* needed me to.

"A little pain play… spanking… bondage. Yeah those are my favorites."

Her eyes narrow a bit. "So why do you have a medical exam bed in your playroom?"

"Yeah, that's not an exam table. That's where I like to play with wax. Wax gets messy and I don't like it near my bed."

I watch as her shoulders go up and down while she breathes. "Yes," she murmurs. "I could see that. But... what do you do with the wax?"

"I melt it, carefully, and paint you with it."

She blinks in surprise. *"Really?"*

"Well, paint might be a stretch. It can burn, so I'm careful, but a little pain enhances the whole thing. You'll see. I'll show you when we get back." I pause. "A little electric play can be hot. Some breath play. Something tells me you wouldn't be game for that, though."

She frowns, her pretty blue eyes fixed on me. "Would that involve those hoods?"

I shake my head. "Not necessarily."

We lay there in the quiet, just the sounds of our breathing and far away another door opening and closing. "Do you want to talk about what happened earlier?"

She doesn't blink or even look away, but keeps her eyes trained on me steadily. "The part where you took your belt to my ass? Or the part where I called you *sir* and begged to come?"

I shake my head slowly. "No, baby." I need to know. How can I protect her if I don't know? "The part when you checked out at the school."

"Oh," she says in a little voice, and now her eyes leave mine. She reaches her hand out to stroke her fingers along my shoulders. With my arms under my pillow, the muscles on my shoulders bulge. Slowly, as if she's stroking a sleeping lion, she runs her fingers along my bare skin. The touch is gentle and sweet. Touching me must soothe her because she doesn't stop the soft stroking while she speaks.

"I was raised in foster care and abused." It surprises me how she speaks without preamble, just telling me exactly what happened. "The last man who was my guardian was principal of the school where I went until high school. He was an evil man." I don't say anything as she speaks, giving her the space she needs to tell me what she needs to, in the time she's comfortable with. "I wasn't his only foster child. He was an angry, volatile person, who took in children to make himself look better. But he hated us. I remember being locked in closets and told that I was stupid and slapped around."

I think of my own sweet Devin, and a flare of anger heats my gut. She continues, still running her fingers along my arms and now my back, tracing the muscles methodically. "The other teachers at the school would back him up. There were no places to go that were safe." She smiles sadly. "So that's why I decided to become an officer."

And look where that brought her. She literally has no safe place, nowhere she could turn to as a child and now as an adult. But she isn't alone anymore. She doesn't have to face this by herself.

"And that's why you need to see justice served," I supply. She hasn't said much, but it was enough.

"Yup."

She takes in another deep breath and lets it out. "I like your muscles," she says with a smile. "You're strong."

She goes to pull her hand away and I take it in mine, bringing her fingers to my lips. "Thank you."

She frowns. "For what?"

"For trusting me. Is there anything else you want to tell me?"

She shakes her head and closes her eyes, and now she

looks as tired as she should be. "Get some rest, Zoe," I instruct. "Sleep now."

Obediently, she closes her eyes, but as I watch, she tosses and turns and can't seem to get comfortable. Finally, I reach for her, draw her onto my chest, and hold her close. Her cheek on my chest, I feel her whole body relax. I stay awake for a long while, holding her, as her soft breathing fades into rhythmic slumber. I don't know how long I'll have with her like this. I want it to last. But there are only so many things I can control.

Chapter 10

Zoe

When I wake the next morning, I feel more well rested than I have in a long, long time. I think sometimes even in sleep, I'm on alert, ready to defend myself if the need arises. But last night… last night, something shifted. He tapped into a part of me I don't ever reveal to others. A soft, vulnerable side of me even I'm unfamiliar with.

He spanked me and fucked me, peeling away the layers of self-protection I have built for myself. Hell, I even told him about the things I don't speak of. I close my eyes briefly. It helps if I can pretend I'm still asleep. I can feel Braxton behind me, my back to his front. His large, warm hand rests on my hip, and when I move closer to him I can feel his warmth beside me. Slow breathing indicates to me he's still asleep, but I won't be able to tell unless I look at him. I let myself relive the night.

The way he unfastened his belt, his eyes alight with determination and intensity. The snap of his belt on my naked skin, the way it burned hot and deep, marking me as his. The way he'd made me climax, my head thrown back and breath frozen in my lungs, my body seizing as I rode the throes of passion and ecstasy.

Then the way we talked, whispering in the darkness, a borrowed place and time where trusts are kept, and hushed secrets given voice. He listened. Then he held me until I fell asleep.

My heart belongs to this man, and I'm powerless to stop it. I'm never powerless to anything. Where do we go from here?

"Morning," he says with a raspy, early morning grumble, and I feel him press more firmly behind me.

"Morning," I say with a giggle. He playfully slaps my ass, then I'm squealing, as his arm snakes under me and I'm lifted straight off the bed and into his arms, then planted belly-down atop him. I can tell by the way his cock presses into my belly that he wants me. Excellent.

"You sleep well?" he asks, tucking my hair behind my ear in what's become his signature move.

"Mhm," I say, smiling at him. Somehow being around him makes me feel soft, the anger curbed in the light of his quiet presence.

"Good," he says, the humor fading from his eyes. "Because today we have a big day ahead of us. Zack called early this morning. You were still asleep, but I took the call."

Wow. I must've really been totally zoned out.

"Did he?" Curiosity bubbles up within me and I try to push away but he holds my wrists fast.

"Uh uh. You're gonna listen, babe."

I nod and bite back the irritation that threatens to make me lost my temper. "Go on."

He watches me carefully before he continues. "Seems Antonia Zandetti's friend unearthed some information involving Senator Malloy."

"You mean presidential *candidate* Senator Malloy?"

"The very same."

"I see." I immediately conjure up an image of Malloy. Red-faced, with heavy jowls and beady eyes, he's bought his way up to the top and managed to pocket big name corporations. I don't know much else about him, except that he has major connections and he's running for fucking president.

"Jesus." I breathe in deep. It seems the corruption runs far deeper than a cop in a local police department. "And what does that have to do with Daniel Zandetti's affiliation with Homeland Security?"

"A lot. Malloy's been accepting bribes to keep quiet on drug trafficking. We don't know how far his connections run, but we do know that Malloy's no innocent, that he was investigated by Antonia's friend the investigative reporter, who went missing at the same time as Antonia."

"So we bring down Malloy," I say firmly, pushing myself so that I can get off Brax's chest and go take my shower. If we're taking down a Senator, I want to move. But before I get far, Brax grabs my wrists and holds me fast, tugging me so that I fall with a little *oomph* back on his chest.

"Not so fast, chickie," he says, which makes me snort. *Chickie?*

"I want to move," I say. "We didn't come here to sightsee, you know." I'm feeling a little irritated, and he doesn't seem to care. Instead, he seems to be paying more attention to me than I feel he needs to. I want him to move his ass and get out of bed so we can get a move on, but instead he's eyeing me with pursed lips. The next thing I know, he's got my hair gripped in his hand and his mouth is to my ear.

"Watch your tone, Zoe."

"Fuck tone, *Braxton,*" I say, throwing his name back at him. He'll get no *sir* from me. He releases my hair, sits up, and pushes me off his chest. "Get on your knees."

A trace of heat ignites low in my belly, even though I feel the need to press on. "What the hell? Let me go?"

"Is that a vanilla?"

I grit my teeth and glare. Hell no.

"The place where we need to go to track down Antonia doesn't open for another hour," he says. "And before we go, I want to be sure you're in a good place."

I blink at him, confused. What's he talking about? He leans down to me, eyes a glacial blue. "Now do you need me to punish you? You need another spanking already? Because if I have to repeat myself again, that's exactly where this will go."

"God, you're an asshole," I mutter.

He parts his legs. "I'll teach you how to use that mouth," he says, a glint of something wicked making me tremble. The embers within me flame to life, and I scoot off the bed and fall to my knees in front of him. I lick my lips. I want to see pleasure in his eyes.

I swallow, as he lowers his boxers and takes his hard cock in his hand, fisting it. The air in the room feels suddenly warm, a trickle of heat tickling my skin at the sight of him pumping his cock.

"Please," I whisper, without realizing what I'm doing I'm closer to him, my mouth at his cock.

"Open." I close my eyes and welcome him into my mouth, moaning a little at the salty taste of him on my tongue. I venture a look at him. His eyes have rolled backward, his mouth slightly parted. Yes. Hell, *yes*. Just as I feel the surge of power I have over him he grips my hair so hard I feel the tug along my scalp while he pumps into me, fucking my mouth.

"Yes, baby. Jesus, Zoe, just like that." I slide my tongue along his thick shaft, loving the power this gives me even as he tugs my hair. The spike of pain shoots right between my legs, and I moan with my lips around his cock, whimpering a little.

"What you gave me last night was beautiful," he says in my ear. "And fuck if I'm gonna let that go."

He pumps so hard in my mouth tears blur my vision, but my heart pounds with every thrust of his hips. The slightest clink of metal warns me before I hear the whizz in the air. Still holding him in my mouth, the lash of his belt reignites the heat on my ass, a line of fire making me throb with need. Jesus *Christ*. He's whipping my ass while I suck him off. I'm heady with arousal, muffled moans coming from my mouth as I work his cock with everything I've got. I pump his shaft and he thrusts into me. I can hardly breathe, before another lash of fire licks at my ass.

"Good girl," he says, his voice thick and harsh. "Don't you fucking stop or this gets way more real."

"Mmm," is all I say, sucking him hard and fast, my hands on his knees as he brings back the belt and lashes me again. I whimper and nearly gag with another savage thrust. He pulls out of me and bends down to kiss my cheek.

"Fucking beautiful," he whispers, before he lifts me up in the air and face plants me on the bed. "Spread those knees. Give that sweet, wet pussy to me."

I do what he says, opening my legs for him just before he plunges into me so hard the breath whooshes straight out of me. I can still taste him on my lips, still feel the pain on my scalp. He slaps my ass with his open palm, a loud crack of flesh on flesh awakening the flames of his belt. I'm on the cusp of orgasm when I feel his hot breath on my neck, his raspy voice demanding and harsh.

"Fucking beg me," he growls. "If you come before I say, you'll go another week before I let you come again, and your ass will be mine."

I whimper with the need to hit ecstasy.

"Please," I moan, tossing my head to the side and arching my back.

Another slap of his palm has me screaming out loud.

"Please *what?*"

"Please, sir!"

He grants me ecstasy with two little words. "Come, baby."

I scream out my release as he roars out his, riding the waves of pleasure that surge through me until I'm flat on the bed, my chest against the bedspread and my mouth parted, panting.

"Good girl," he says, pushing aside my dampened hair to kiss my cheek. "*Now* we go take the shower." He pulls out and I feel him get off the bed. Strangely, my throat feels clogged with tears. What just happened?

I shift to get off the bed, but a sharp slap to my ass freezes me in place. "Stay there while I clean you up. I'll tell you when you may go to the bathroom."

I hear him padding to the bathroom, then a moment later he returns with a warm, damp cloth. He slides it between my legs and cleans me off. "That's a girl," he says. I peek out of the corner of my eyes to see his stern face watching me carefully. I smile. He smiles back.

"That's my girl," he says. "My good girl. There she is. Now up you go, we're off to shower."

What does he mean? I'm the same girl I've always been. I might *feel* a little different but I'm still the same. Still, we need to move now. I want to close in on what we need to do. I need to see Antonia Zandetti with my own eyes and get to the bottom of our purpose here. So I follow him out of bed and to the bathroom. Showering with him feels like the most natural thing in the world. I find myself loving how he takes care of me. He soaps up a washcloth, and when I reach for it, all it takes is one firm shake of his head to tell me *no*. It's not so hard to let him take care of me now. Not after last night and this morning.

He runs the washcloth over my shoulders and back. The warm water steamy, mingled with the pungent, soothing scent of lemongrass fills my senses. He lathers up my hair then gently tips my head back until the water runs clear. He cups his hand around my eyes to shield them from suds. When we're good and clean, he gets out before me, towels off, then wraps the towel around his waist before lifting another large one and holding it out for me.

"Step into it," he orders.

Without really even thinking about it, I do what he says, letting him towel me off. He takes a second towel and dries my hair. I'm still not used to how light it is, how easily it dries. "Come on, now. Let's get you changed."

I feel as meek as I ever am. I like it. A little voice whispers to me that I'm letting him in too far, too soon, but I don't want to listen to that voice. It's nice, feeling safe like this, but I have some questions.

We slip into a comfortable silence, as he pulls on his clothes and hands me mine.

"Brax?" I have to ask him.

"Mmm?" he asks, then he reaches for his belt and threads it through the loops on his pants. I swallow, my mouth dry at the memory of what he did with that belt.

"What are we doing here?"

He raises a brow and a corner of his lips quirk up. "Tracking down Antonia Zandetti and finding out intel on Malloy, so we can find out who the fuck is after you," he says. "And I'm also starving, so breakfast has to be somewhere on that agenda."

"Right," I say, turning my back to him. My throat is tight, and I swallow the lump down. That's why we're here. There can't be more to that. He's a man with a child, and I'm not fit to be a mother. I know this. And yet...

"Zoe." His voice carries an edge of warning to it. "Why did you pull away from me like that?"

I shake my head. No. I'm not playing games with him. If he's going to reject me and what we just did doesn't mean to him what it means to him, I don't want to know. Not now. Not yet.

"*Zoe.*"

A sharp tug on my arm makes me spin around to face him. I blink and look up at his eyes, blue storm clouds with a hint of gray.

"What?" I whisper.

He grips both my arms and pulls me against him. "We're here to track Zandetti. But last night, you submitted to me. This morning, you did the same. And when you do, I get a glimpse of that soft, beautiful woman behind that tough-as-nails exterior. The one who will stop at nothing to protect the innocent. And the one who has a fucking hard time letting anyone take care of *her*."

I swallow.

Oh my God.

That's what this was about?

"Oh," I whisper. "But I just mean... where does this leave... *us?*"

Without warning, he releases my arms and tugs me close to him so that his lips meet mine. I melt into the kiss, letting him claim me in silence, until he pulls me away. "Today, we find Zandetti. You stay with me and we work this through." He takes in a deep breath. "Tomorrow, we find *us*. Deal?"

I smile. I'm not really sure what he means, but I respond almost instinctively. "Yes," I breathe, smiling up at him, I give it a shot. "Yes, sir."

Chapter 11

Brax

I watch from the corner of my eye as she takes a large bite of the bagel smeared with cream cheese we picked up from a local coffee shop. It's bigger than her head, but she's making short work of it.

"Seems getting fucked hard works up an appetite with you," I tease, taking a sip of the scalding hot coffee. It's got a nutty edge, dark and robust, and I welcome the heat down my throat. I need to be on my game with the day ahead. We're four miles out from a little boutique where Antonia Zandetti supposedly works now. I got in touch with Myers before we left, and he gave me the specs of the place. Stock room in the back, small staircase that leads to a basement, escape route in the stock room if necessary.

"Hey, dinner last night is but a distant memory," she says, swiping at her lips with a napkin. She misses a spot, so her tongue darts out to lap up the bit of cream cheese still there. I swallow hard, remembering what magic she does with that tongue. Christ, I can hardly stand the way she unravels me. I haven't been with a woman like her. I've been with submissives, but have stuck mostly with scening at Club Verge. Something about the whole 24/7 thing seems oppressive, like maybe it'd get boring after a while. I admire the guys who do commit like Tobias and Zack, but from a distance have always sort of mourned the freedom they relinquished when they put on those rings.

But now… I don't know where things are going with Zoe, but I do know that she brings out things in me I never expected. The idea of her being apart from me, or with another guy, of even being on her own again without me by her side, makes me sick. Having her submit to me makes me feel like a fucking king, like I rule the world, even if I have to fight my way there.

I reach out for her hand and squeeze. "We're almost there," I say.

"Well, are you gonna eat your breakfast? Gotta fortify yourself before you go kick ass," she says. She lifts my sausage and egg burrito and peels back the wax paper it's wrapped in, handing it to me. I smile to myself and take it from her.

"Thanks." I take a bite, my mind a million miles away. She's suffered, this woman, and even though she's an adult now, the wounds inflicted in her childhood run deep. I'll never forget the haunted look in her eyes she got when we were in Devin's school. I wanted to lift her in my arms, tuck her into my chest, and run with her, away from the demons that chased her. She doesn't trust easily, and she doesn't let down her walls for just anyone. She's done that for *me*.

But now we've got shit to do. "When we get to the boutique, we case it. Myers says there's a stock room in the back with an emergency exit if we need it, and a basement is storage. There are three employees, and Antonia's boyfriend is the owner, though of course she goes by another name now. She's Carolyn to everyone who works there."

"Got it." She wads up her paper and sits up straighter, patting her side. "Tucking your sig into the waistband of your jeans sucks balls compared to a holster," she says with a grimace.

"Wait. What? You brought your fucking gun?"

She rolls her eyes and tosses her hands in the air. "You think I'd go in unarmed? Are you fucking kidding me?"

I growl to myself. I suppose she has reason to bring a weapon, but still. *Jesus.* That ups the stakes here.

"Wait a minute," she says, eyeing me warily as I cruise to a stop at a stoplight. "Don't tell me *you're* unarmed."

I huff out a breath. "Of course not." I've had a license to carry for a while now, and I won't go on a job for Myers without protection.

"So it's okay for me, a trained officer, to go into a high risk situation with nothing to defend myself but my hands and mouth? What am I supposed to say, 'Stop! Hold your hands up, or I'll shout again?'" She's shaking her head, but still I can't help but snort out a laugh. She has a point.

"Just means I need to keep a closer eye on you now, though," I say. The light turns green and I watch the dot on the GPS move as I accelerate. One mile out.

"I can handle myself," she retorts, the edge in her voice returning.

I reach for her leg and gently squeeze her knee, a reminder to her to listen to me. "I never said you can't, Zoe. But you're with me now. And there's no beating me off anymore. Got it?"

She tries to pull away.

Yeah, like I'll let that happen.

My grip on her tightens, and I intentionally move my hand further up her thigh, knowing it'll get her attention.

"I'm not gonna let you pull away from me, Zoe. You let your partner protect you?"

Reminding her of the man that could have lost his life may not be the smartest move, but I need to make my point.

"Of course I did," she says, a little of the tension in her waning. I hear her swallow, so I gentle my voice.

"It's no different. I'm here to protect your ass and you're here to protect mine. We've got each other's backs. That's all. Okay?"

She lays her hand atop mine on her leg. "Yeah. Of course." There's more that needs to be said but now's not the time. "Just… make sure you're not holding me back. Seriously, Brax, I'll kick your ass if you do that."

I pull into an empty parking space on the street, not too far from the boutique. I can see the silver and red awning from where we sit.

I've never had a submissive threaten to kick my ass before. I'd like to see her try. Hell, I'm hard as a rock just thinking about it. But is she a submissive? Who the hell knows. All that matters is that she's Zoe, we're in this together, and she's fucking mine.

"You try to kick my ass, I'll pin you over my knee and spank *your* ass. Deal?"

She shakes her head and rolls her eyes, but a faint pink flush colors her cheeks. "*Fine*. Deal."

Win for me.

"This is the place," I say. "You go in and pretend you're a customer. You'll find out who Antonia is, and make small talk. We'll have to get her alone to get the information we need, but I'm not sure how easy that will be."

"Right," she says. "Pretend to like shoes and shit,

pretend to be nice and sweet, and then once we find her we close in."

My lips twitch upward. Reaching over, I give her midnight black hair a quick, sharp tug, watching her eyes heat. She loves that even if she narrows her eyes at me, as if daring to take her further.

I fucking love her feistiness.

"Yeah, babe. Something like that."

Once we get out of the car, we check to make sure we look like normal civilians, weapons completely secured. My phone's in my pocket and she's got hers in hand. We walk side-by-side to the door, and I open it for her, the jangle of the bells alerting the occupants inside that we're here. She goes in first.

It's warm in here, and the space is fairly small. Circular displays showcasing what looks like handmade shawls and scarves with bold floral prints edge the periphery, and in the center, small tables with jewelry stands are front and center. Zoe goes straight to the bracelets on display, fingering delicate silver shells as she cases the small enclosure, eyes flitting discreetly every which way. I can feel the tension in her body as she observes everything. She's alert, ready to act, intelligent as fuck. A flicker of pride hits my chest.

"Hello." Zoe looks up, and a young woman with blonde hair in a braid that falls over her shoulder smiles at us. Not Antonia. "Is there anything I can help you with?"

"Hmm," Zoe says, contemplating the bracelet on the stand. "These are so pretty. But I'm wondering if you have these styles in gold, not silver?" She looks over her shoulder at me. "My boyfriend favors gold." Her lips curl up. "And he's paying."

So we're playing that angle? I can roll with that. I smile at the clerk. "She's not *allowed* to wear anything but the best. Isn't that right, sweetheart?" I place a hand at the small of her back and pull her closer to me.

"Of course," she says with a grin.

"I see," the girl says, nodding. "Let me go back to the store room and see what we have." Both of us eye the door, looking for any signs that Antonia is about, but when the store room door swings open, all I see is blackness.

"You see anything?" I whisper to her.

She shakes her head. "Nope."

I'm beginning to wonder if we've hit a standstill when the door to the shop jangles. I turn to see an older woman with dark skin enter the store on the arm of a much taller man. She's changed her hair and wears glasses now, but there's no mistaking Antonia. The man she's with bends down and kisses her cheek, then makes his way to the store room.

"That's her," she whispers in my ear. "And her boyfriend."

I nod. Bingo. Now we just need to get them to talk.

"Hello," she greets, shrugging out of a sweater. "Are you two being helped?"

"Yes, thank you," Zoe says. "I was reading about this shop on Yelp, and it seems you get some of the highest ratings of any boutique on the Cape." She smiles up at Antonia. "It must be the stellar customer service and the exceptional quality of your products?"

Antonia smiles. "Perhaps. We do aim to please. Please let me know if there's anything at all I can get for you."

Zoe nods once. "Thank you."

We need to make our move. Not twenty-four hours ago, the man Zoe partnered with was attacked. Here stands the woman who has answers, and we're not going to fuck around. Zoe looks at me, our eyes meeting in mutual agreement, before she places the bracelet down and steps to the counter. I follow behind her.

"Actually, there is something you can get me," she says, her smile fading. The woman's eyes grow wary, but we advance on her so that her back is to the wall where leather wallets and keychains hang. She has nowhere to go. Zoe keeps up her friendly, conversational tone. "I'm actually looking for some*one*, not some*thing*."

"Oh?" the woman asks. Her eyes dart to the stockroom, and the door swings open, but just the blonde emerges.

"Oh, Carolyn, there you are," the blonde says. "Do you know if we carry the shell bracelet in gold?"

"I'll have to check the stock room," the woman says, sidestepping so that she can get away from us. There's no way we can let her get that far. If she does, she'll escape, and we lose our lead.

"No," the girl says. "There's nothing there. I already checked."

Her smile is plastered on her face as she responds, facing us, and walking quickly to the back room. "Oh there are a few storage places that I can only access with the key." She's lying, trying to escape as her steps quicken. We need to make our move *now*. I nod to Zoe and jerk my chin toward the door. She steps quickly ahead of Antonia, blocking her exit, and walks up to her as she yells up to the girl in front. "Can you find the straw hat right near the entrance in a small for me?"

"Of course," the girl says, stepping further away.

Now that Zoe has the woman cornered, her voice cuts through the quiet like a whip. "Antonia Zandetti." Zoe's eyes blaze into Antonia's, her stance prohibiting any movement. "We're not here to hurt you, but you need to listen to us. Send your employee out on an errand."

Anotonia's eyes shutter. "I have no idea who that is," she whispers, taking another step toward the stock room, but now I'm following right behind Zoe, caging Antonia in.

"We're not going to hurt you," I say, my voice calm and smooth, meant to placate. "But do as she says now."

The woman shakes her head. "Get out of my store before I call the police," she whispers, her hand clutching at her throat. Her eyes are wide, nostrils flared.

"Antonia," Zoe whispers, stepping even closer. "We're here because the police are the ones after you. Now get rid of your employee so we can have a little chat."

"You're lying," Antonia spits out.

"You have until the count of ten," I say. "That's one."

She blinks.

"Two." Her eyes dart from the room to the storeroom. "Three." I've learned to use the power of numbers in high-stakes situations. It usually has the desired effect. "Four." I raise my brows at her, giving her my most formidable dominant look. "*Five.*"

"Chelsea!" she yells out, her voice a bit strangled. I do feel badly for her that she's afraid, but this was the woman who covered her own ass when her husband was killed, after cheating on him. She went into hiding with information that could've convicted those who deserve prosecution. People are dead because of her.

The blonde in the front looks back at her, startled. "Yes?"

"Please do me a favor, and fetch me a latte from the little coffee shop down the street? And get yourself whatever you'd like. Put it on my account."

"Certainly," the girl says. "Anything else?"

"Just the latte," Antonia orders.

"No problem. I'll be right back." The door clangs shut behind her. Zoe removes her gun from her hip, the silver flashing. Antonia's eyes widen. Zoe points her gun at the door.

"Go lock the door."

Antonia does as she says, heads to the door and clicks the locks in place, but on her way back, she sidesteps toward the checkout desk.

"Oh no you don't," I say. In two long steps I reach her, but it's too late. She's hit a red button, and a noise sounds in the back. I grip her arm and haul her to the room with me, nodding to Zoe as I tug Antonia forward quickly.

"Open that door and look out." Antonia's man is right behind the door and *fuck*, he's been alerted something's wrong. Zoe nods, her sig now chest high, and opens the door. I push Antonia through in front of us, hoping to stall her boyfriend, then follow suit.

Predictably, the man's lunges himself at us, but she quickly dodges his advances with a duck, wraps her arms around his chest, and yanks him back. He's burly but she's nimble so she quickly gains ground. He stumbles, so she knees his back, making him go sprawling. Antonia's made a run for the door, but I'm faster. I dive after her, grabbing her arm just before she yanks the door open. She screams and pulls, trying to get away, but I hold her fast, tug her into my chest and wrap my arms around her. I restrain her and eye Zoe. She's got one knee on the big bear of a man on the floor in front of her. He's pinned in place, and she's panting, but everyone seems otherwise unharmed.

"We're not here to hurt you," Zoe says, cutting her eyes to the woman I'm holding in my grasp. "But we need answers."

"Fine," Antonia says. "Let me sit, and I'll tell you everything."

With my left hand, I remove cuffs from my pocket, push her out in front of me, and snap them on her wrists. I slide my finger underneath the metal, making sure she's got enough room to be comfortable. "Sit," I tell her. I help her slide into a chair by a small circular table. I nod to Zoe, giving her the green light to take over.

She cuffs the man on the floor, then helps him to his feet. "Same. We're not here to hurt you. But we need answers."

He nods, and Zoe leads him to the seat beside his wife.

Zoe stands in front of them, hands planted on her hips, and angles her body so she blocks the exit. Her eyes go straight to Antonia. "Your name is Antonia Zandetti. Your former husband was murdered, his body found in the Central Park Lake. You know who killed him and why," she says.

"How did you find me?" Antonia asks, her face pained and pale, despite her dark olive complexion.

"That's inconsequential at this stage," Zoe insists. "Our time is limited. Those who killed your husband came after me in my own home. I was forced to go into hiding when I found out information involving Officer Ben Hoffman." She looks carefully at Antonia, whose eyes widen with recognition. "We need you to tell us what you know, so that we can track down every single guilty accomplice affiliated with Hoffman and Malloy."

Antonia swallows, looks at the man sitting beside her, and he nods.

She sighs. "And how do I know to trust you?"

Zoe looks at me. Identifying herself as an officer puts her at risk. What she's doing isn't even close to legal, and could cost her her badge, and in this situation, worse. I give her one shake of my head. *Don't do it. Don't tell her.*

She looks away, and for a moment I worry that she's going to give away her identity. I take a step toward her involuntarily, as if to defend her if she puts herself at risk when she pulls out her phone. She swallows hard, her hands trembling, as she swipes at the screen, and pulls up footage of the car bombing. There was a video that went viral online. I want to tear it from her hand and stop it, but it's too late. Flames flicker on the screen, news footage scrolling below the photo.

"This was a car bomb yesterday meant for me," she says. I can tell by the firm yet somewhat strangled sound of her voice this is costing her to divulge this information. "The man injured here was an innocent who was in the wrong place at the wrong time. He could've been killed."

Antonia winces and looks away, but Zoe closes the space between them. "If I wanted to hurt you, Antonia, I would have already done it." To my surprise, it's her boyfriend that speaks up.

"I'm sick of hiding here, pretending we don't know anyone or anything." He looks to Antonia. "If these people can help us put the men who killed Daniel Zandetti behind bars, we need to tell them everything we know."

Antonia's gaze swings to Zoe. She straightens her back and lifts her chin up.

"Yes," she says, her voice rough and husky with emotion. "It's time."

Chapter 12

Zoe

WE'RE HEADING BACK to our hotel room; the sun is high at mid-day. It's breezy and mildly warm, and I want to take a walk. How safe are we, though?

Brax has been on the phone for what seems like hours. First, he called Zack, and told him everything, then he set up an appointment with Myers for when we return. I sit in the passenger seat, listening, digesting. Antonia and her husband have left to stay with Antonia's sister north of the Cape until a safe house is secured for them by Myers. I've promised them we'll be in touch when we have more intel. Now it's time to dig.

Antonia confirmed Hoffman's affiliation with Malloy. The person who knows the final pieces to this puzzle is Mona Kingsley, the investigative reporter who went into hiding. Antonia won't give us her whereabouts but says that she'll have her friend contact us.

And that's what we need. We need to find that woman,

get the read on what she knows, and take down those who are after me, Antonia, and whoever else they suspect are threatening their livelihood. My head is spinning as Brax pulls to the side of the road. To my right, just outside my window, waves crash to the shore, the skyline dotted with fluffy white clouds. It's sunny and bright and so carefree, belying the danger that lurks in the shadows. My mind goes back to the footage I played for Antonia, the flames on the screen so vivid I could almost feel them myself. The memory makes nausea roll in my belly.

Brax hangs up his phone and tosses it on the dash. "Done a good day's work, officer," he says with a smirk.

"Yeah? We're nowhere closer to finding the people behind all this than we were before." I turn my body away from him but keep my gaze steady. How can he look so amused when people are dead?

Brax shakes his head. "We get the call from Mona, and we pursue that lead. It's the next course of action here." He leans back in his chair. "This we know. Your man Hoffman's on Malloy's payroll. Malloy is running for president, and his affiliations are less-than kosher. We know Antonia, in league with Kingsley, dug up information on Malloy that threatened their lives. Antonia's husband went down first. The other two women were assumed missing, but it seems they escaped."

I nod. "Right."

"Hoffman's working with someone who's paying him, and that someone is paid by Malloy. We also know that."

"Right."

"So we're not exactly in the dark, here," Brax says with a smile. "We just need to put the pieces together." He reaches over and tugs my hair. "How are you holding up?"

I pull away. "I'm good."

Fuck tenderness. I want to find out who's behind all

this. I need to put them behind bars. I need to be able to walk free again. Hell, I need Antonia to be able to walk free again. No one should have to hide, afraid for their lives.

Brax's phone buzzes, and he grabs it off the dash. He shakes his head. "Just Myers."

He takes the call. "Yeah, man. No. Can't give you that information over the phone. I'll tell you what I know when I see you. Yeah, we found her. You get the names of those involved with Malloy?" He purses his lips and shakes his head. He huffs out a breath. "I'll tell you as soon as I know." He shuts off the phone.

He turns to face me, frowning. "Myers is a pain in the ass. Jesus, we need to close in on this." He looks at me, and there's nothing but honesty in the blue pools of his eyes before he continues. "I want this behind us, so we can move on to bigger and better things."

The implication makes my heartbeat stutter. I swallow hard. "Oh yeah? Like what?"

He smiles at me, reaches over, and tugs a lock of my hair, but though he's teasing there's a glint in his eye I'm learning to crave. "Like your training."

Oh hell no. "My *training?* I'm well trained, *sir*," I respond, giving him the *sir* with an edge that defends my position and hardly defers to him.

Now frowning, he flexes his arms and his nostrils flare. I swallow as his biceps bulge. For a brief moment, I wish that we weren't here for the reasons we are, that he was mine and I was his. That we were on a vacation. I want that. I want to walk this beach in front of us and welcome the sand between my toes, go buy fish and chips on paper plates at a seafood place, then go back to our hotel room and get to know Brax a little better. Let him know me. End the night curled up in his arms, where I feel safe and comfortable in my own skin.

I swallow. That's not why we're here.

He rubs a hand across the stubble on his chin. A siren wails nearby. It's coming closer, and we're suddenly both at attention. But then my phone rings, and I look at the screen. The number is private. Looking at Brax, I answer.

"Hello?"

"Zoe McKay?" I nod, even though whoever belongs to the soft, feminine voice on the other end of the line can't see me.

"Speaking."

I hear her blow out a breath. "I'm Mona Kingsley. Antonia says you've found us, and you're on Malloy's trail."

"Yes," I say, using my calmest voice to hopefully keep her speaking. "I won't pose a threat to you."

She pauses, and I close my eyes. She's the one we need. Without her, we can't move forward.

"Even you can't keep me safe," she says, the terror in her voice prickling my skin. I sit up in my seat, take the phone from my ear, and silently hit the speaker. I watch Brax as she speaks.

"Mona, I'm here to put the people in pursuit of you behind bars. I'm not here to hurt you. Can you please tell me where I can find you so that we can talk?"

Her voice trembles. "What do you want from me?"

"I know that Senator Malloy has the NYPD in his pocket." Giving her full transparency is the only way to garner her trust. "I know you and Antonia unearthed incriminating evidence against him, and shortly after that her husband was killed. I know that Malloy is running for president and has people on his payroll that cover his hide. But there are a few more things I need to know before I set into motion the actions that will end the threat to you, Antonia, and hell, all of us."

There's a pregnant pause. "Fine," she whispers. "Set up a private conference call for tomorrow morning to make sure we aren't tapped, and I'll tell you what I know."

"Mona, I—" But she's already disconnected the call. I look to Brax. His eyes meet mine and he gives one firm nod.

"Let's go back to the hotel and set this up with Myers. We check out and head to Verge tonight." I nod, and even try to think up a reason that he's wrong, so he doesn't get to call all the shots here, but he makes good sense. "I want to be sure that we've got everything in place before we call her, and that we're safe. You already know why I think Verge is the best place for that."

A part of me wonders if he wants to get back to Verge because that's where he's in his element, where his toys and tools are. Where he's in utter control. Where it's safe.

I look at Brax. Even he isn't safe anymore, and it's all because of me. It isn't fair that he's got to take precautions because I've put him at risk. He's a good man, and he has a daughter. And even if we *weren't* in danger, I'm not the kind of girl a man like him should end up with. He needs to be with someone who can help him parent his daughter. Someone who knows all about submission and how to meet those needs of his. Someone without a fucked up past like me.

At a stop light he meets my eyes, probing.

"You've got that look in your eyes," he says.

I shake my head. "You haven't known me long enough to decide when I have a 'look in my eyes.'" I toss up air quotes to show him he knows fuck all about this. About *me*.

"Bullshit," he says, reaching out to place a firm hand on my knee as he accelerates. Apparently, this is his dom move when we're driving. "I'm a dom, sweetheart. Doms learn quickly how to read emotion. The best doms use that knowledge to meet the needs of a submissive. If you're pushing me away, it's for a reason."

"Yeah, whatever, Brax." The thought that he thinks he knows me annoys the fuck out of me.

I shove his hand off my knee, just as we pull into the parking lot of the hotel. His jaw set in a firm line, he allows me to push him off me as we pull into the parking space just outside the entrance where we need to go. "Don't get out," he says. "I'll come around and get you."

What the hell is this power move? We've got shit to do. I remember what he did the night before, though, and how he brought me to surrender. As he comes around to my side of the car, I have a silent internal battle. Defy him, and risk pushing him away? Or defy him, and bring that dom out in him that I crave? Or… do what he says, and see where obedience takes me? My teeth clench as I wrestle with the choices, and just as I've decided fuck this, I'm getting out, the passenger door swings open and his large hand is outstretched. Waiting for me. Guiding me out of my seat.

I blink, not sure how this makes me feel, but I'm left with few choices now. Not meeting his eyes, I take his hand. I let him lead me. I let him hold my hand, just for this brief moment, and pretend that I'm his. What does being his mean? Do I give up freedom of choice? Does he tell me what to do, control who I interact with, demand my undivided attention?

I don't know. And not knowing scares the hell out of me.

When we reach the door to our room, I tug my hand out of his. Surprised, he only blinks at me, then taps the entry key and lets me in. After I step over the threshold of the door, he gives me a sharp slap to the ass, ushering me into the room.

"What the fuck?" I say, heat rising in my chest. "Anyone could've seen you. Who the hell do you think—"

He shuts the door behind him with finality, grabs both of my wrists, and pins them to my side, before his mouth crashes down on mine, a hard, punishing kiss that pushes the air right out of my lungs. Flames gallop across my chest and down my belly, a low throb of need pulsing between my thighs. Jesus. *God* this feels good. He's solid, resilient, immovable. Here's a man that takes what he wants without detracting from who I am, what I want. Somehow the loss of control I feel at his mercy is exactly what I need.

Still, I need to push him. I need to flail out against him and know that he can take me on, that he won't let me push him away. That when I storm against him he won't wither or fade but stand strong when I need to fight. There's a beast in me that isn't placated by kindness, a ferocity that needs to wail and gnash its teeth at times. I won't hide that part of me from him. And hell, something tells me that even if I tried, he wouldn't let me.

"Let me fucking go." Even as I say the words I know I don't mean them. If he let me go now, I'd lose the respect that he's earned from me in the past few days. I'd never be able to look at him the same way again. The backs of my knees hit fabric and I fall back on the bed, bouncing upward as he looms over me. My pulse races in my veins, my cheeks flush with the whisper of excitement and energy his strength holds over me.

"Let you go?" he asks, his knees hitting the bed on either side of me, caging me in. "I'm not holding you. Who's holding you back, Zoe?" His voice is low and controlled, but a muscle ticks in his jaw as his hands fall on either side of me. The heat of his body surrounds me, making my belly dip with sudden arousal. "You're a fully trained officer. You could have me on the floor and immobile if you wanted me there. I've seen you do it." He leans down to me, his breath tickling the delicate skin at my neck. "Are you telling me no? I need to get you to Verge sooner than later. I'll teach you that saying no to me gets you punished. Is that what you want?"

"Brax," I breathe. I close my eyes, my voice trailing off as I whisper. "Jesus, you can't keep doing this to me."

"Doing what?" The sound of his voice at my ear makes a delicious shiver run through me. "If you don't like this, you safeword. You know that."

I don't want this to stop. I just need to be able to push back.

I shove my hands up, only to have them trapped and pinned by my sides. I squirm, fighting so hard my abs contract and my arms burn. I push against him, needing to feel how immovable he is. Needing to know he isn't budging.

Jesus, *God*, I never met a man like this.

"You want me to stop this?" he flutters kisses along the edge of my jaw, down my neck. "You can make this stop anytime you want to. But you know what, Zoe?" I squirm and push him, but he holds me fast and barely budges. His mouth comes to my ear, drawing the lobe between his teeth, sending a flare of pain along the tender skin. His hot breath skates across my flesh. "I think you like this."

I can't push him with my body, but I can push him with my words. "So, what? You have me on my back, pinned down. What does that prove? That you're stronger? Big fucking deal." It seems I've crossed a line, as the next thing I know he tilts me to my side before whacking my ass with the flat of his palm, once, twice, three times. I squeal but he holds fast.

"Something else to say, little girl?"

I shake my head. The small spanking makes my pulse race, my clit throbbing with need.

"Good." His sharp voice makes me freeze in place. "You. Stay. *Right. There.*"

Still focused on the burn of his palm on my ass, I can't even think about doing anything but listening. I freeze, waiting for his next move. I hear the clink of metal and the whir of a belt through loops, and briefly wonder if he's going to use his belt again, but then he's on the bed kneeling again, the leather at my wrists. With a jingle and click, my wrists are fastened above my head. I blink at him in bewilderment, not expecting this move.

"Close your eyes," he instructs in a low, steady purr. Obediently, I shutter my eyes, welcoming the dark surrender. With my eyes closed and my wrists secured, I focus on the sounds around me. My breathing and his. A car far in the distance honking. The ice machine clinking outside our door, followed by the harsh caw of a crow and a flutter of wings. I'm still fully clothed, and I become aware now of the weight of my jeans, the hem of my t-shirt that's ridden up hitting my belly.

He starts with gentle fingers on my scalp, the tips drawing through my hair and massaging gentle circles at my temples. I sigh in contentment. Though he's only touching my head, it's as if he's drawing out any stress or residual anger I felt. The tender massage grows heated as his fingers entwine in my hair and tug, lifting my head as his mouth comes to my ear.

"Your only job right now is to obey. Do you understand me?"

"Yes."

The pull on my hair intensifies. "Try that again."

"Yes, sir," I breathe. *Yes, sir.*

Fabric caresses my eyelids, soft and warm. Gently, he lifts my head and nimbly fastens something behind my head. He's tying whatever it is so that I'm effectively blindfolded. I try to open my eyes, but I can't. I'm encased in darkness, held in place with his belt, and at first, I feel a rise of panic. I tug at my wrists and squirm, my head flailing from side to side. His deep voice cuts through the panic like a beacon in the fog.

"Stop."

I freeze.

His voice softens, stroking my skin as softly as the fabric over my eyes. "Good girl."

My heart squeezes at that, the gentle praise possibly even more effective at keeping me obedient as his harsher manner.

A warm, sensual tickle at my temple tells me he's kissing me, his scent enveloping every bit of my senses. "You're so beautiful," he whispers in a harsh whisper. "So fucking beautiful." His hands smooth up my sides as if holding me in place. I can't move away from him, can't get out of his grasp, held in place underneath him like this.

I like that I can't.

Nimble fingers are at my waist, unbuckling my jeans. "Slide 'em off," he orders. He tugs them down, and I help him by lifting up my ass. He slides the pants past my hips, down my legs, then off one foot at a time until I hear the soft swish of fabric falling to the floor. I gasp when his mouth finds my panty clad pussy, planting a heated kiss at its center. He presses his tongue on the fabric, right where my slit is, the damp fabric clinging to my sensitized skin. When I feel him tugging down my panties, I begin to pant.

"Brax," I whisper.

"Mmm?"

I say nothing, truly not knowing how to respond.

"Just relax," he says, before he places a gentle kiss to my belly. Somehow, the kiss warms me through. I smile to myself. I like doing what he says.

Just relax.

I give myself over to the feel of his mouth on me, and when he pulls down the edge of my panties, I'm lost to the sensation. Every slow, gentle stroke of his tongue melts away a little bit of my resistance until I come, my pelvis rising while he holds me, stroking ecstasy from me like a master musician with his instrument. Panting, I fall to the bed when he releases me, welcoming him at my entrance with a gentle part of my thighs.

His mouth at my ear, he breathes the words his own need palpable. "Who does this pussy belong to?" I can feel him at my entrance. My body tenses with the sudden need to have him deep within me, that closeness that literally nothing else can fulfill.

"You," I breathe, needing to submit myself to him in this moment. When the blindfold is off, and my wrists are free the magic is lost. Here, where it's dark and I'm quiet, I can give him everything and lose nothing. The air in my lungs vanishes with the first savage thrust of his cock.

His voice at my ear, he asks another question. "Who does this mouth belong to?" The pad of his thumb traces my lips as he thrusts, and I instinctively kiss the calloused skin.

"You."

He builds a tempo, silently asking for surrender with every movement of his hips, our slick bodies merge as one, whispering what needs to be said when words fail. He tenses, on the cusp of climax as my own body heats and coils, needing to chase my orgasm with his. I know what he's going to ask next, and I don't know if I can say it, but my body does.

"Who do you belong to?" he rasps.

My body crashes into climax speaking the words I can't utter but need to.

You.

The blindfold's damp with tears as he holds me tight. We lay in the quiet aftermath of our bliss, his fingers tangled in my hair. He reaches behind my head, tugs, and light fills my world again. He's smiling down softly at me. Tenderly, he bends down and brushes a kiss to the top of my head, then lowers his mouth to my temple. "You're crying, baby," he says. He kisses a tear away. "Are you okay? Did I hurt you?"

There are so many things I need to say but can't.

He isn't the one making me cry.

He's the one who hurts me in a way that frees me.

I shake my head. "I'm good. Let's go to Verge." We need to finish this once and for all.

He's so close, I can see the flecks of gray in his blue eyes. I can tell there are questions behind that gaze, but he won't push further and hell if I don't love him for that. He nods, one quick nod of acceptance, then pulls out slowly. Still tethered by his belt, I wait for him to clean me, then release my wrists. He dresses me next, slipping on my panties, then my jeans. My wrists are free now, and I could insist on dressing myself, but I like the attention and gentle ministrations.

For now, I'll let him take care of me. It's something he needs, and today, I'll give him that, before I need to slip away. I'll never forget this, though. Brax is the first man who has ever shown me the beauty of a gentle giant.

Even when I'm gone and I'm not his anymore, I'll carry this with me.

Chapter 13

Brax

SHE SLIPS in and out of my fingers like fine silk, rare and priceless, buttery soft but resilient. I try to hold onto her, but I can't. In her moments of submission, I see the woman who lets me in, the vulnerable side to her that yearns for the protection I can give her. But when the moment fades, she sets her face like flint, an instinctive mask I'm not sure she even knows she wears.

We need one commodity we don't have right now: time. What she doesn't know is that I don't give up as easily as she thinks I do. I'll give her the space she needs to sort things out, but I've glimpsed my prize, and I'm not letting go. I don't want a woman who's supple and compliant. I want to fight for her submission and earn it, like a king in battle. I want all her flaws and imperfections with her beauty, for it was in overcoming her demons she became who she is today.

"I'm starving," she says, kicking her feet up on the dashboard. "Dude, you know how to work up an appetite."

"I'm flattered. Burgers?"

"Perfect."

I pull into a drive-thru and order food, and a few minutes later we're on the road. She tears into her burger like she hasn't eaten in weeks, douses her fries in ketchup, and shoves four in her mouth at once before she slurps from her drink. After this, she daintily swipes at her mouth and sighs with contentment.

"Let's do dinner the right way when we get back. Next week. You like Italian?"

Looking out the window, she shrugs. "Not much in the line of food I don't like."

"Me neither." I reach for her knee and squeeze. "And you didn't answer the question."

I pull onto the highway as she turns back to face me. I can't see her eyes, but I can feel the sharper tone. "I'm not sure how to answer that question," she says. "I'm not sure what we're doing here. Are you asking me on a date?"

"Yeah," I say. "We were sorta thrown into this, and now I want to do things the right way. Woo you and all that shit."

She snorts and shoves my hand off her knee. "*Woo* me, like you're some sorta Shakespearean hero? I don't know, Brax." Her voice gets flinty. "I was sort of under the impression we were fuck buddies."

Jesus. The phrase hits my gut like sudden nausea. "Is that right," I say, feeling my own hardness surface.

"I don't know," she says. "I honestly just don't know. I mean, I like you." Her voice shakes a little, betraying her. "But I'm fucked up, Braxton. Like, seriously fucked up."

I reach for her hand and squeeze it. "What makes you think you're any more fucked up than the rest of us?"

She doesn't answer but traces the bumps of my knuckles with delicate fingers. "You have a daughter," she finally states in response.

"I do." Devin is my priority and she knows that isn't changing.

"And… I don't know anything about daughters. Or kids. Or… things like that."

I nod. It's a fair concern, and one I can't dismiss. I was warned about her baggage before we even met, but hell I'm the one who brings complications to the table.

She shakes her head with a self-deprecating laugh. "See, this is what I do. You want dinner and I'm already thinking I can't handle a kid. I mean, it's not like you asked me to marry you." She tries to pull her hand away, but I won't let her. I hold on tight, and place her hand right back on her thigh, under mine.

"You're right. I didn't ask you to mother my kid. I asked you on a date. But I like the fact that you're thinking ahead." There's something between us I've never felt before, a gut instinct I can't ignore. Deep down inside I know: when she pulls away, I have to tug her back. "I'm not in this to be 'fuck buddies.'" She flinches when I throw her phrase back at her, telling me silently that she hates the idea as much as I do. "As far as my daughter, I get it. But she already has a mother, baby. I'm not asking you to fill that role."

"I couldn't," she whispers. "It's not… that I don't want to."

"And that's not what we worry about today."

She nods her head. There's a brutal honesty that fuels this woman, so when she nods her head, I know she's doing so in acceptance of what I'm proposing. "You're right," she says. "That's not what we worry about today.

Today, we get our asses back to Verge and bring those motherfuckers to justice."

I grin. She's gritty as hell and I fucking love it.

"Hell yeah," I say, and without another word, I accelerate. Today, we need to get to Verge. Talk to Mona Kingsley. And slam the asses of the guilty in jail. Tomorrow, we work on us.

EVERY COUPLE that's interested in each other needs a five-hour road trip. Two rest stops later, we've talked about the music we listen to, the high school shenanigans we pulled, her ex-boyfriend who took her virginity and told everyone they knew. She won't give me his number so I can track him down and kick his ass, but I can tell the idea amuses her.

I tell her about Nichole and how young and stupid we were, and she grows real quiet when I recount Devin's birth, and how holding that little baby for the first time was my introduction into being a real man. Knowing I had more than myself to look out for. We talk about how Nichole and I fought to make it work, but it was doomed from the start. Nichole mocked my dominant ways in bed, called me a freak and a pervert when I attempted anything kinky, and finally left in the middle of the night and moved in with her parents. It took me a full year to get over that while I fought for visitation with my daughter. Now, we have our boundaries, and I make her respect those.

It wasn't until I met Tobias and Zack when they founded Club Verge that I came into my own. It was the first time in my life I met people who understood the way I was wired, who helped hone my skills and not mock them.

"I have to admit, I thought kinky shit was really fucked

up," Zoe says, leaning back in the chair with her feet up on the dash.

I shrug. "Hell, maybe some of it is. But there's something for everyone."

"What do you like?" she asks.

"Submission." I answer without giving it much thought.

"I mean *kinks,*" she says, though she pulls a bit closer to me. "And I'm not fucking submissive."

I huff out a laugh. "Baby, I know. Believe me. But I said I like *submission*. When did I say anything about a submissive personality?"

She grows quiet, a small smile playing at her hips. "I like that. So someone can submit part time?"

"All depends on the couple. And there's a difference between part time submissive and submitting to *one person*."

Fuck, I want to be the one who earns that from her.

The rest of the drive to Verge is like coming home. I try to tell myself not to hope, not to dream. But Zoe MacKay makes that impossible.

Chapter 14

Zoe

I WAKE THE NEXT MORNING, my mind racing. The ride home yesterday with Brax was like dating on speed. What's freaking me the hell out is that I haven't held anything back from him. I've let it all hang out. There's something about being tied up and spanked that'll do that to a girl, I guess, draw out the fears and honesty unlike a regular fuck or make-out session.

I watch him as he sleeps, his broad shoulders rising and falling with slow, unhindered slumber. He's facing me, and I smile to myself at how relaxed his face is. The worry lines between his brows soften in sleep, and he doesn't carry the weight of the world. He's the kind of guy that needs to carry things, to protect and lead and defend. But here, while he's lying here with me, I can see the vulnerability in him that makes him human. I go over what he said yesterday on the car ride home and remind myself.

There's a difference between being a natural sub and submitting to one person.

I fucking love submitting to him. It's as natural as breathing, and hot as hell, and even though I'm not exactly sure what it all encompasses, I'm game to try.

That's not what we worry about today, he said. He's not going anywhere. Today, we bring these assholes *down*.

My phone vibrates on the table. I reach for it and slide out of bed. My heart beat kicks up when I realize the number belongs to Mona. She's calling earlier than I expected. I glance over at Brax, who's still dead asleep, grab the phone, and slide into my shoes. I'm wearing boxers and a t-shirt, so I walk quickly out of the private room and into the main club. It isn't until the door closes behind me that I remember it automatically locks. I turn around, reach for the lock, then swear when I feel the familiar solid handle. My phone buzzes again. One more ring and the sucker goes to voicemail.

"Hello?" My voice sounds louder than I expect in the quiet. Verge is vacated this early, but I still feel exposed as hell.

"Hello?"

"Yeah. Mona?"

I hear the confirmation on the other end of the line. "Yeah."

"I can't talk long," she whispers. "I need to confirm the names you need to find and tell you how you'll bring them down."

"Yes?" My heartbeat races. I look quickly around the room but see nothing but the vacant bar. I need to write this down. Jogging, I head to Tobias' office. I know he's got paper and shit in there. "Hang on, I'm just getting something to write this all down. Okay?"

"Okay."

Thankfully, Tobias never closes his office door. It's still wide open, and right there on his desk lies a few pads of lined yellow-paper and a coffee mug filled with pens. I sit at his seat, feeling a little guilty at the invasion, and click open a pen.

"Hoffman's in league with Malloy. You know this. Malloy is on the payroll of drug lord Taras Sokolov, but the man you really need to bring down immediately is Joseph Benton."

The blood runs cold in my veins. "Benton?"

Benton's my boss, the chief of police.

"Yep. He's the one behind Hoffman, and the two of them bury the information, all incriminating evidence that proves Sokolov was hired by Malloy to kill Zandetti.

"And if I do this, what evidence do I have to convict them?"

She gives me the details of a lockbox she has secured in the heart of NYC, then gives me the information I need to obtain. It's perfect. Everything I need.

"Thank you," I say, adrenaline pumping through me. I need to wake up Brax and we need to get things done. "What can I do for you to help you?"

"Nothing," she says. "No one knows I'm alive. I'm safe. You bring these men down, and I'll do what I need to get this into the press."

Something catches my attention as she speaks, quick movement out of the corner of my eye. I blink, turning to look at a string of cameras Tobias has mounted on the wall to the left of his desk. Security feed that leads to every entrance to Verge. Two men dressed in black are heading past the entrance and to the back door. It's still dark enough outside so I can't see much, but I'm on my feet, watching. "Thanks, Mona." I wish her the best and thank her again, needing to end this call. These men are coming into this building, and I need to see where.

With the skill befitting a master thief, one slides something silver near the lock, shimmies it, and I watch in fascinated horror as the door swings open. But I'm no fucking wallflower. I'm a trained officer, and these assholes aren't going down without a fight. I know intuitively they're here for me and for Brax. We stirred something up this weekend. Hoffman's found us.

I look wildly around me. I have no weapons, nothing to defend myself. I realize then how much harder it is to face danger without the weapons I've come to rely on. My sig's next to my bag in Brax's room.

Brax!

I leave Tobias's office and stand at the entrance to the bar, listening. There's a sound of splintering wood and shouts. They found him. *Fuck.* They're in that room now, with Brax, and when they get him they'll kill him.

I take off at a run, weapons be damned.

"Where's the bitch?" I hear Hoffman's voice and someone else's. "Where the fuck is she?"

"I don't know. Jesus, I have no idea." Brax's voice is strangled as if he's in pain, and a rush of anger momentarily blurs my vision. If they hurt him, I'll fucking kill them. I've pursued assailants so many times I've lost count, but never, *never*, has anything been so personal, so pressing. They're threatening *my man*.

I'm the she they're looking for. I look wildly about the vacant hall. If I come in through the entrance to the room, I'm fucked. No weapons and in clear sight of the men in that room.

"You know where she is. You're hiding her. Where the *fuck* is she?"

I hear Brax cry out, and panic wells in my chest. They're hurting him. Fuck, they're going to kill him. Realization dawns on me like a flash of lightning. There's a bathroom into the private room. If I could get outside, climb up, and get into the bathroom that way, I can sneak attack when they're not expecting me to. I race as fast as I can out the exit, circle round the building, and make it to the window outside of Brax's door. Thankfully it's the same level as the street. Last night, Brax opened the window to let some fresh air in. Thank God. Any further tinkering and I'd be screwed.

I open the window, thankful for my small size and limber frame. Hoisting myself in feet-first, I slide in and quickly fall to the floor on the pads of my feet, as nimble as a cat. I listen, my stomach twisting with the sounds of flesh hitting flesh. I'll fucking *kill* them. I look wildly around me for something, anything I can use as a weapon. Hanging in the shower is a long bamboo bath brush with a loop on it. I snag that, run to the door and take a deep breath. Now's my chance.

I open the door and scream like a wild animal, hoping to attract attention. I take advantage of the momentary stunned silence to drop to the floor, seconds before gunshots ring out. They're so close to me I can almost reach them.

"Son of a bitch," Hoffman growls, lunging for me, but I dodge his attack and swipe at his legs with the bath brush. He howls, gripping his leg, and falls to one knee. I whack him a second time, when a gunshot rings out, followed by a flare of white pain in my leg. I'm shot. Fuck, someone hit me.

Hoffman recovers, and I push myself up, grab him by the chest, and heave him in front of me like a shield as a second shot rings out. Hoffman's garbled scream tells me the target's hit his mark. I release him, drop and roll away from the gunshots, just as Brax hurls himself from the bed and tackles our assailant to the floor. His open palm crashes into the man's jaw, making his head snap back, before he knees him in the groin. The man howls, but Brax is pissed. "You fucking shot her. You son of a bitch. You *shot* her." He punches the man again, blood spurting from the guy's nose, then a second punch and the man's head lolls to the side.

"Brax!" I shout, trying to get his attention. He reels his head to look at me. I jerk my head toward the bedside table, where he houses his cuffs and ropes. He gets me, and with a quick nod, opens the drawer. He removes a pair of gleaming silver cuffs and tosses a pair to me, before he snaps the second pair on the guy he's restrained.

He grins at me across the room, one eye swollen shut, his lip split wide open, and it strikes me then how this whole situation fits us. I saved *him* and he saved me. We're bloodied and bruised, but survivors, the two of us. We'll see justice served, and we won't give up. We'll do it together.

"We convict these two for breaking and entering and assault and battery first," he says, picking up his phone. "I'm calling Zack."

I nod. "Got the call from our contact this morning." I grin at him. "All's a go." We have everything we need.

He grins at me, warming my chest like sun breaking through clouds. "We do."

I know exactly what he means.

Chapter 15

Brax

"NO MORE FUCKING PAIN MEDS." Zoe's jaw is clenched and she's looking at the doctor as if he just suggested she cut off her arm. His gaze swings to mine. The guy looks like he's barely out of high school, clean-shaven and clean-cut, wearing small round glasses perched on his nose and a pinched expression. He's about six inches shorter than I am and needs to look up to speak to me.

"She needs pain meds," he says. I find it amusing he wants me to make her take them. I fucking love her defiance. Hell, I'm practically getting hard just watching her spar with him.

I nod, my arms crossed on my chest as I watch her. "Why does she need them?"

We've been here for four days, and in lockdown in intensive care for the first four days. That had nothing to do with her injury, which is fairly minor, a simple graze of the bullet that stung but didn't injure. Zack and I wanted to be sure she was safe, and ICU was a better option than even a private room. Security monitored her door as well.

Three days later, Zack and his team recovered the information from Mona Kingsley, and in an epic takedown that made the local news, the chief of police and Hoffman have been arrested, and even Malloy is now being held without bail. I wanted Zoe safe, so the ICU it was.

"Gunshot wound victims who spent time in the ICU will frequently need pain meds to aid in recovery," he says, exhaling an exasperated breath.

"That's great for them," Zoe says. "I don't want them."

She isn't looking at him but me, though, as she throws off her covers. "And I've waited three hours for my discharge papers. Can we get that moving?"

He looks at me again. He was here the other night when she refused to eat her dinner and I pretty much dommed her into doing what she's told. She's not the most cooperative of patients. She wants to be home, back to work, and ready to take on whatever she needs to, and is tired of being holed up in this place. If I think she needs to behave, I'm fine with making her. Hell, I crave it. But now isn't one of those times.

I showed her triumphantly the news reports of the arrests that were made, and she even received a sweet personal letter from Mona. But she shook her head. She isn't satisfied to sit around and let others do what she thinks is her work.

"If she doesn't need pain meds, she won't take them," I say to the doctor. "Zoe can handle herself and is smart enough to know if she needs to resort to meds. I won't make her."

He frowns. Finally, he blows out a breath. "Fine. I'll send the nurse in with your paperwork." He shuffles his papers and goes on his way.

"Honest to God," she mutters. "You'd think I was refusing something important."

I pull up a chair next to her and sit down heavily. "Some would argue that is important, Zoe."

She looks into my eyes and she isn't angry anymore but pleading. "It's... look, I don't like how I feel on them. I don't like how they mess with my brain, you know? I'm not even sure that makes sense, but I feel less in control of myself when I'm on them, and I don't like that."

I can understand that. Nodding, I reach for her hand. "Fair enough. I understand that totally. So, no pain meds, but you'll promise me that you won't let your pride get in the way of you taking care of yourself." I give her the stern look that usually squelches the storm in her eyes. "Deal?"

"Deal." She smiles, her face brightening, and my heart gives a little twist.

I want to say something corny and sappy like, "Where have you been all my life?" but Zoe doesn't dig sappy, and it isn't me anyway. Instead, I reach for her hand and squeeze. She takes my larger hand in hers, holds it up to her chest, and squeezes back. Sometimes words aren't really necessary anyhow.

A short while later, she's walking out of the hospital with me. The superficial bullet wound she sustained patched up easily. She's got a crutch for now, until she's comfortable enough to bear weight on her injured leg, but I know she'll ditch it within days.

"I can't believe I'm really free," she murmurs to me. "Hoffman gone. Malloy. All of them, on his payroll. And all for what? A little drug money?" She shakes her head. "It's disgusting."

"I know." I reach for her hand and take it in mine, enjoying the feel of her warm skin. She doesn't say anything, and I wonder what she's thinking. The two of us have been thrown together in a crazy, intense situation beyond our control. And where are we now?

"You ready to go back to your place?" I ask, leading her to the passenger side of my car while I hit the unlock button.

"Hell yes," she says. "I cannot *wait* to get back and have some privacy again," she says. "Eat in my own kitchen. Sleep in my own bed." She pauses and turns to me. "Can you help me get my things, though, from Verge?" My stomach dips at the thought of all her things no longer taking up space in my private room at Verge and her retreating. It means the end of something that we only just began.

I need to make a move.

"Yeah, of course," I say. "I'll help you get all your stuff, under one condition."

I usher her into the passenger side of my car then walk to my side and slide into the driver's seat.

"Yeah?"

"Yeah. You have to promise you'll come back with me to Verge at some point. As in, I take you as my guest," I say to her, turning to see how she takes this news. "Like a date. In fact, I want that to happen this weekend. Sound good?"

She flushes a faint pink, and her eyes warm. "Yeah," she says. "I'd like that a lot. Actually, I was sort of hoping you'd ask. It almost got to the point where it felt like a second home." Grinning, she holds up a finger. "*Almost.*"

We sit in comfortable silence while I drive her to Verge. After a while, she pipes up, her voice softer than usual.

"So. Brax?"

I look at her briefly and nod, my mind a mile away. In a few weeks, Devin has her ballet recital, I got another call from Myers, and I'm on for dungeon monitor at Verge tonight.

"Yes?"

"Now that the people who were after me are behind bars, I want to know. Where does that leave us?" Her voice shakes a little, which surprises me. The entire time, during this whole damn ordeal, she kept her shit together. Her voice didn't waver, and she never shed a tear. But now, here we are at a crossroads, and she needs to know where this leaves us. Pride swells in my chest, knowing she wouldn't have asked me if this didn't mean something to her.

If *I* didn't.

But there's one thing she needs to know.

I'm not letting her go.

I don't care if it takes months or years, I'm not giving up until she knows that she's mine. I'll tell her now, and I'll tell her tomorrow. I'll tell her when she wakes up in the morning and when she goes to bed at night. She'll hear it in my words and see it in my eyes and feel it in my touch, until the conviction runs through her like blood runs through her veins.

Zoe MacKay fucking belongs to *me*.

"Where does this leave us?" I ask. "It's taking everything I have not to take you into Verge so I can claim you. Mark you. Keep you where I can watch you every second of the day. If you can't handle that, sweetheart, we're gonna have to have a talk."

The corner of her lips twitches up. "Yes," she says softly, then her voice rises in pitch and she turns to face me. "*Yes.* Forget taking me home. I want to go to Verge now."

Though she amuses the hell out of me, we need to establish some ground rules.

"Zoe." She sobers and tenses at the deeper sound of my voice. Good. She's learning.

"Yes?"

"If you're with me, we have to have an understanding."

She's a multi-faceted enigma, a beautiful, heartbreaking meld of past, present, and future, intricately woven with needs I yearn to fill. She longs for the empathy and companionship of a friend, the protection and guidance of a dom, the thrill and adoration of a lover.

I'll be that man.

"Yes?" she repeats.

My voice is hoarse, roughened by the eagerness that claims me. "For starters, that would be a *yes, sir.*"

Her answer will pave the way for me. Can she handle my demands? Trust me enough to yield to me?

Squirming in her seat, she leans over to me as I pull on the road that takes us to Verge. Will she contradict me? Change her mind? Tell me she needs to think things through?

But no. I cruise to a stop at a red light and swing my gaze to hers. Lips parted, she nods with eagerness. "Yes, sir." she whispers. Voice trembling a little as she speaks, her fingertips flutter at her throat. "I have no idea how to do this, you know."

My chest swells, the road in front of me wide and open.

She said yes. That was all I needed: the simple trust and reassurance that she wants this as much as I do.

"That's where I come in," I say, with pride. "I'll teach you."

Chapter 16

Zoe

I'm not the girl who gets all mushy around guys. But Brax is different, bearing a sort of protective honesty about him that other people don't have. When he opens the door to Verge and the bouncer at the door eyes us, Brax grins with me on his arm. "Got my girl with me tonight," he says, his voice taut with pride.

His girl.

Hell, I'm a mess. I don't have any makeup on, and I'm still wearing the rumpled clothing I changed into before I left the hospital, but I'm grinning like a kid on Christmas.

He wants me. I'm his.

His arm skirts around to my back, and he flexes, pulling me close as he leads me to the entryway that ushers us into Verge. "I need to freshen up a bit," I say, just before we enter the bar area.

"I can help you with that," he says, waggling his eyebrows at me. I can't help but snort, even as heat flares across my chest at the thought of what he'd do to help me.

"Zoe?" I turn around to see Zack and Beatrice coming

in the main door. My jaw drops. Beatrice is dressed in a teeny tiny little number that barely covers her ass, with a pair of fishnets and death-defying platforms. A tight leather collar with silver studs graces her neck. A flush of pink colors her cheeks. Zack is dressed head-to-toe in black, an amused smile playing at his lips. I knew these two were members here, but I've never seen them in full attire.

"Yeah," I say, turning to them. "I just got released, and Brax brought me here to pick my things up." I hide a smile that would reveal the truth in my lie. We're not here for a simple errand. I can't help but smirk a little at them. "Aren't you two cute?"

Brax gives me a playful smack to the ass.

"Hey, I'm not judging. I might want to borrow those shoes…"

Beatrice laughs out loud. "Welcome to Verge, Zoe," she says, her voice rich and warm.

I know what she means. Even though I've been here before, tonight is different. This is the night I walk in here because I want to, not because I'm drunk and horny, or because I'm running from criminals, but because what I need is here. Beatrice swishes past me and gives my arm an intimate squeeze. She leans in and whispers, "Welcome to the family."

A lump rises in my throat but I swallow it, as Brax grips my hand.

Then Zack and Beatrice are gone, absorbed inthe crush of people on the dance floor outside the club.

He leads me past the bar, and Travis and Tobias greet us as we walk past. I know every detail of this room and the next, but tonight I feel like this is my first time gracing these halls. When we reach the door to his room, I have a strange sense of the familiar and unknown dancing with one another. I know this place. But it almost feels like I've never been here before.

The door swings open, and he ushers me in. When the door shuts behind us with a click of finality, I spin to say something, something snarky and lighthearted to alleviate the building pressure in my chest, but I forget what I'm going to say when his lips meet mine. He bends, hands under my ass, and lifts me. My legs wrap around his torso, my chest up against his, as he carries me to the bed, never breaking the kiss. He drops me on the bed and I bounce a little, but then he's on me, knees trapping me in, the heat of his gaze pinning me in place. He doesn't need ropes and cuffs to bind me.

"Strip," he says, a hoarse demand that makes me quiver as he pulls the hem of his shirt and yanks his t-shirt right over his head.

I nod. "Yes, sir." Jesus, it feels good to call him that. My fingers fumble taking my clothes off, the sounds of zippers and fabric rustling filling the quiet room. When I'm bared to him, he kisses me from my jaw to my neck, holding me so tightly it almost hurts, but I need that possessive touch. Gentle right now would be an insult.

He runs his hands over my body as if he's making sure I'm not going to evaporate, a firm pressure of calloused palms that sends a shiver through my body. "Get on your knees," he orders, his mouth to my ear. "*Now.*"

He removes his hands just long enough to give me a motivating smack to the ass. My chest falls to the bed, arms stretched in front of me as he's taught me, ass in the air. When his body comes down flush against mine, I'm overcome by his scent, musky and heated like burning embers. Fisting my hair in his hand, he yanks my head back, sending a delicious tingle down my spine before he spanks me, a hard smack of his palm on the swell of my ass, igniting the fire only he can quench.

But tonight, he doesn't reach for his toys. There are no cuffs or bonds or playthings to bring me to ecstasy. We don't even speak words, as if the vibration of our voices would somehow invade our privacy. Tonight, we only feel.

I close my eyes when I feel him press against my slit, clenching the blanket when he thrusts into me, a silent claim of body and will. He fills me, my pussy clenching around him, my breasts swelling on the bed as he pounds a rhythm of brutal pleasure. My need builds, somehow bridging the chasm of pain and pleasure, then he whispers in my ear. "Come with me." Not *for* me as he usually says, but *with* me. He wants to chase our ecstasy as one.

"Yes," I breathe, startled to feel dampness on my cheeks. "Yes," I repeat, my voice cracking under the weight of my hope and fear. Then stars blind my vision and I'm soaring while his grip tightens painfully. He moans his release as I ride the waves of our mutual pleasure. Time loses its meaning. I'm floating, numb with pleasure, weakened beneath him.

Our breathing slows now, the gentle chorus of my breath with his abating. He pulls out of me and rolls over. We're sweaty and messy, but I don't care. I need to feel his arms around me. Snuggling up on his chest, I close my eyes when he holds me tightly. I listen to the soft, steady pounding of his heart beneath my cheek. I'm sore where I was injured and tired from not having enough sleep at the hospital, but I've never felt happier in my life.

"Stay with me," he says, and I remember when he said that to me before. I know he means more than my physical presence. He won't let me pull away and hide who I am. He sought me out, found me, and treasures what he found.

Not the shiny new, spiffed-up version of me, but the

scarred one. The tarnished one. The real me. The one who pushes him away even though the thought of separation kills her. He keeps coming back for me, and hell if I don't love him for that.

I take a deep breath and I close my eyes. I can't bear to look at him when I say what I need to. If he rejects me now, I can't bear to see it. Finally, with a deep breath, I utter the words I've never said to anyone in my life. I've never known anyone who deserved them.

"I love you."

I'm startled when he grabs my chin and yanks it up, my eyes flying wide open. "You look at me when you say that," he growls.

He won't let me hide.

"I love you," I repeat. Before he responds his lips press mine, a firm but gentle reassurance that tells me what I need to hear.

Pulling away, he still grips my chin, the fiery blue of his eyes piercing me. "And I love you," he says, before he breaks out into a grin, revealing that dimple I've adored from day one. "You can run but I'll always catch you."

I smile, at peace now that I've faced the fear of those words and survived. "For the first time in my life, I don't want to. There's no need to run anymore. I've found where I needed to go."

Epilogue
SIX MONTHS LATER

Brax

TOBIAS WHISTLES, shaking his head as he finishes reading the article I handed to him. "Jesus, man, that was one hell of a first case," he says with a chuckle. I laugh with him. He's right. It sure as hell was quite an introduction into the world of private investigation.

Zoe grins up at me with pride shining in her eyes. We've spent every day together since that night I took her home from the hospital. She's gone back to work, now that Benton and Hoffman are behind bars. Malloy is under arrest, thanks to a top-notch investigation led by Stefan Myers, fueled with information from Mona Kingsley. Antonia Zandetti's shop on the Cape was closed, and Mona has led us to believe that Antonia and her husband have moved to a place somewhere in the Mediterranean.

"You gonna keep up this P.I. work?" Tobias asks.

I nod. Myers pays me well, and I like the work he gives

me. Nothing's been as intense as the work I've done with Zoe, but that's fitting.

She's special.

"And you're still on the force?" Tobias asks Zoe.

"Of course," she says, the smile fading. "Why would I leave the force?"

God, I love her feistiness.

"Oh, I don't know," I say, tugging a lock of her hair that's grown a lot longer since the short cut Beatrice gave her. "Maybe it's time for you to settle down and get all domesticated. Wear aprons and bake me some pies."

Her eyes flash at me but she can't hide the way her lips twitch. The idea of Zoe baking me pies is ridiculous. I'm the one that does the cooking since I moved into her place, and she's totally fine with that arrangement. Hell, Devin says I make the best tacos she's ever had.

"Playing with fire," Tobias says to me. Hell, he's right though. That's why I love her. She's playing with fire.

"Gotta go," I say, pushing to my feet. "We're on our way to Devin's recital." Zoe stands, and I brush a thumb over the raised marks on her wrists she has hidden with a delicate ivory long-sleeved top. I know what's beneath that top. Crisscrossed rope marks under her breasts and over her belly, wrists lightly pink but still bearing the mark of our play before we came here. I have a shibari demonstration later this week, and she's allowed me to practice on her.

It wasn't a hardship.

She loves my ropes, my cuffs, and the pain and pleasure of a spanking. Slowly but surely, I'm introducing her to more intense sessions, the marks on her body now testimony to the well of trust she's let me build. One of the members here is a kink therapist, and Zoe has been going to her. It's not easy. Sometimes she comes home from her sessions emotionally wrecked, but it's not unlike her sessions with me. They bare her pain but make her stronger. I hold her and tell her I love her. Every time she goes, she's that much stronger.

We leave Verge hand in hand, and head to Devin's school. Zoe loves going with me to see Devin now. She isn't Devin's mom, and she never will be. But she's a positive, loving presence in Devin's life, and I fucking love her for that.

"You know, it's been six months," I tell her, when I cruise to a stop outside of Devin's school.

"Yeah?" she says with surprise. "Wow. It seems... weirdly shorter and yet longer."

I nod. I feel the same, as if I've always known her but we only just met.

I turn to face her and reach for her hand. It's not a candlelight dinner and hearts and flowers, but Zoe's not into that. She likes things simple and straightforward, so that's what I'll give her.

"Six months, and yet it feels like forever," I say, letting the words hang in the air with meaning.

She nods. "Exactly."

I suddenly need to say the words, so she hears the conviction in my voice and knows I mean this. "So let's make it forever."

Her brows arch and her lips part. Jesus, she's beautiful. So fucking beautiful.

"Forever?" she whispers.

I can hardly breathe, needing her affirmation of this. "Yes," I manage to choke out. "Forever. Will you be my forever?"

She grasps my hands and squeezes, then takes me be surprise when she bursts out laughing. "Yes. Hell *yes.*"

I join her laughter and take her mouth with mine.

Her answer is perfect. Just like her.

THE END

Bonus material

Chapter one from Deliverance *(an NYC Doms standalone novel)*

"You son of a bitch," I hiss, intentionally keeping my voice low. Crazy, half-cocked, vindictive ex-lover isn't normally my thing.

Hell, there's a first for everything, though.

"Diana! *Stop.* This is stupid, and girl, you *know* I know stupid when I see it because I've done *all the stupid* in my life." Beatrice pleads with me to think twice as she shuffles toward me, trying to place her small frame between me and the car I'm about to destroy.

"Stop the lecture." My hands tremble as I hold the keys, glaring past my blonde-haired, blue-eyed bestie, and focusing my hatred on the silver Maserati. I march past Beatrice, and before I can change my mind, dig the tip of my key into the gleaming exterior with maniacal glee. Crouching down, I take grim pleasure in destroying the most beautiful car I've ever looked at. Sat in. Been fucked in.

"Did you tell Little Miss High and Tight your sob story?" I cackle to the car as if it's my ex-boyfriend embodied. I'd only just met the guy a few weeks ago, my first real boyfriend since my ex-husband took off, but I'd managed to convince myself he was *the one*. My savior. My hero. With a particularly vicious swipe, I lose my footing and nearly sprawl onto the snowy sidewalk, but I catch myself on the bumper. Wind whips at my hair, icy snow lashing my bare skin, but I hardly feel it.

Tequila for the win.

"Diana," Beatrice cajoles. "You've had too much to drink. God, woman! Get ahold of yourself! You've done it, okay? You've done enough. I shouldn't have let you out of the car. This isn't *you*. You're too smart to pull this teenaged shit. Just get in the car and I'll—"

"Leave me alone." I love this girl to death, but I don't trust myself not to shove her out of my way if she tries to stop me. I scrape the key once more, so deep it feels like fucking nails on a chalkboard, but I like knowing the damage will be severe. "You don't know what it's like to walk into your bedroom and see some bitch with her lips wrapped around your boyfriend's cock."

Scrraaape.

"You don't know what it's like to see betrayal in the eyes of the man who said he loved you."

Scraaaape.

"You don't know what it's like," my voice catches on a dry sob, so I underscore my angst with another cut of the key, "to have to explain to your son that the bastard who promised to take him to the drive-in movie theater was a lying piece of shit who'll never come back."

Scrape, scrape, scraaape.

Sitting back on my heels, I eye the destruction with triumph.

Beatrice talks to me like one might speak to a rabid animal, her hands outstretched in a gesture meant to calm. "I may not know those things, but I do know that—" She freezes, her voice now panicked. "Oh. Oh, *shit*. Diana, stop. Oh my *God*. We have to go."

But before I can respond, the deep growl of a man's voice right behind me—a voice *I do not know*—makes me nearly stumble.

"What the *fuck* are you doing to my car?"

Shit.

His... car?

I turn, my cheeks hot despite the freezing cold, to stare into the terrifyingly furious face of the biggest man I've ever seen. He towers over me, even wearing my tallest spiky heels, and the involuntary step I take back helps me see him better. Everything about him is dark, with his swarthy skin and nearly-black hair, but it's his eyes—black as coal beneath thick, heavy brows, that pin me in place. I can't move. I can't speak. I can barely think.

His jaw, covered in thick, dark stubble, tightens when his huge, muscled arms cross his expansive chest.

In any other time or place, I'd find the man sexy as fuck. But now?

"Your car?" I whisper.

"My car," he says in a low growl. "What are you doing to *my* fucking car?"

I blow out a breath and close my eyes.

I'm screwed.

<u>Deliverance</u> *is now live in the Amazon store.*

Stay in touch!

FREE READ!

Sign up for Jane's newsletter and get a free read! Sign up _HERE_.

About the Author

USA Today bestselling author Jane Henry pens stern but loving alpha heroes, feisty heroines, and emotion-driven happily-ever-afters. She writes what she loves to read: kink with a tender touch. Jane is a hopeless romantic who lives on the East Coast with a houseful of children and her very own Prince Charming.

Have you joined my Facebook reader group? We have exclusive giveaways, cover reveals, Advanced Reader Copies, and visits from your favorite authors. Come on over and join in the fun! Join the Club!

Amazon author page
Goodreads
Instagram:
https://www.instagram.com/janehenryauthor

Keep in touch!

www.janehenryromance.com
janehenrywriter@gmail.com

Other titles by Jane you may enjoy:

Contemporary fiction

NYC Doms

Deliverance

Safeguard

The Billionaire Daddies Trilogy

Beauty's Daddy: A Beauty and the Beast Adult Fairy Tale

Mafia Daddy: A Cinderella Adult Fairy Tale

Dungeon Daddy: A Rapunzel Adult Fairy Tale

The Boston Doms

My Dom (Boston Doms Book 1)

His Submissive (Boston Doms Book 2)

Her Protector (Boston Doms Book 3)

His Babygirl (Boston Doms Book 4)

His Lady (Boston Doms Book 5)

Her Hero (Boston Doms Book 6)

My Redemption (Boston Doms Book 7)

Begin Again (Bound to You Book 1)

Come Back to Me (Bound to You Book 2)

Complete Me (Bound To You Book 3)

Bound to You (Boxed Set)

Black Light: Roulette Redux

Sunstrokes: Four Hot Tales of Punishment and Pleasure (Anthology)

Westerns

Her Outlaw Daddy

Claimed on the Frontier

Surrendered on the Frontier

Cowboy Daddies: Two Western Romances

Science Fiction

Aldric: A Sci-Fi Warrior Romance (Heroes of Avalere Book 1)

Idan: A Sci-Fi Warrior Romance (Heroes of Avalere Book 2)

Manufactured by Amazon.ca
Bolton, ON